Who's Grace?

Who's Grace?

JAMES R. COGGINS

MOODY PUBLISHERS
CHICAGO

Library of Congress Cataloging-in-Publication Data

Coggins, James Robert, 1949–
Who's Grace? / James R. Coggins.
p. cm.
ISBN 0-8024-1764-7
1. Winnipeg International Airport—Fiction. 2. Journalism, Religious—Fiction. 3. Winnipeg (Man.)—Fiction. I. Title.

PR9199.4.C64W47 2004
813'.6—dc22

2003016325

1 3 5 7 9 10 8 6 4 2

Printed in the United States of America

For Jackie,
who introduced me
to murder mysteries
and many other things

Chapter 1

SUNDAY, JUNE 16

It was one of those cloudless early summer days when things on the ground were perfectly clear but far away. Below and ahead of the plane lay the city of Winnipeg, the eastern "gateway to the Canadian prairies." A city of less than a million people camped at the conjunction of two meandering rivers, it seemed a bump on the broad expanse of flat prairie. As the plane moved closer, the city rose as an uneven pyramid on the vast flatness, sloping up from the scattered houses on the edge of the suburbs to the bank towers at the city's core.

The pyramid grew and flattened as the plane circled over the first suburbs, the houses appearing as tiny rectangles of color, like houses on a Monopoly board. Behind each house and separated by lines of board fence were slightly larger rectangles of green yard or the green and brown stripes of a garden. Sometimes the green rectangles contained smaller blue and gray rectangles.

The plane circled lower and the green rectangles grew to

matchbook size, with tiny quarter-matchstick figures moving about them. In one of the blue rectangles, a half-dozen such figures gyrated, splashing silently.

In another green rectangle were two matchstick figures. One, dressed in dark clothing, pointed a matchstick limb toward another figure in a white dress near a house. The figure in white jerked its limbs suddenly and leaned back until it was lying on the ground, face up toward the circling plane, its mouth opened enormously wide.

In the green rectangle next door a smaller matchstick figure, perhaps a medium-sized dog, ran around and around.

In another rectangle two matchstick figures reclined on tiny white chairs.

In still another . . .

What had he seen?

John Smyth tried to jerk his tired mind back from the dispassionate reverie which took in the scene below without really seeing. It had been a long conference.

What had he seen? Could it really be that vague impression that was playing around the borders of his consciousness? Was it too unbelievable to think? Yet John Smyth was an expert in things thought unbelievable.

The plane circled lower now, the flight attendants already seated, awaiting arrival. Smyth looked around at the other passengers. They seemed bored, restless, distracted. Had any of them seen what he had seen—what he *thought* he had seen? And had he seen anything at all? His mind was tired, a bit dazed. It seemed to be moving very slowly.

The plane banked, turned, slowed, and dipped. Still his mind would not move. The runway came up to meet the plane with a bump. All the time the plane was rolling to a stop at the terminal, his mind struggled to grasp that vague impression.

The passengers were unbuckling their seat belts now and retrieving their luggage from the compartments overhead. The flight attendants with tired efficiency were opening the doors and giving those wide empty smiles that said, "I'm glad that's over," while their lips were mouthing, "Have a good day."

Smyth picked up his briefcase and camera bag and stumbled toward the exit slowly—at a snail's pace an inch at a time. Whom should he tell? He stumbled past the vacant smiles of the flight attendants and down a narrow corridor in a long, turgid river of people. He turned a corner, passed through a glass door, and began descending some stairs. In the large, crowded room below him, people stood clustered around carousels waiting for their luggage.

At the far end of the room stood a policeman in a blue-and-tan uniform, one of the Royal Canadian Mounted Police officers regularly assigned to airport duty. Smyth hesitated, then slowly approached him. Without preamble, he stopped in front of the officer and stammered, "I think . . . I've just seen a . . . a murder."

"Where?"

"I'm not sure," Smyth replied.

Eventually he was taken to a small room, where he told his story to two skeptical policemen.

"What part of the city was this in—what neighborhood?"

"I—I don't know."

"How long before the plane landed?"

"Five minutes. . . . I'm not sure."

"What was the house like?"

"Uh . . . a rectangle, a house . . . It had a fence."

"What color was the house?"

"I don't know. From my angle . . . I saw the roof."

"What color was the roof?"

"Roof-colored . . . gray? I don't remember. I was watching the people."

His statement was recorded. The senior policeman, a Sergeant Prestwyck of the Royal Canadian Mounted Police, stood up. And up. The man was at least six feet tall, maybe two hundred pounds, with a slight middle-aged paunch and close-cropped hair

"Thank you for coming to us, Mr. Smyth," he said.

Smyth was reluctant to leave. "But . . . what next?"

"We will keep your report," said Sergeant Prestwyck.

"But what will you *do* with it?"

Prestwyck peered down at Smyth. "We will keep your report and put it with whatever other information we receive."

"But aren't you going to look for the murderer?"

"Mr. Smyth, we don't really know that you saw a murder. You saw two tiny figures near a house in a backyard somewhere in Winnipeg, doing something. That's just not much for us to go on. If there has been a murder, there will be other evidence. There will be a body. Or someone will have heard the shots, and the police will already be there. Thank you, Mr. Smyth."

Smyth shook his head as he was ushered out of the office. There had been a coolness in the sergeant's voice ever since that brief interlude when the sergeant had seen the nametag on Smyth's briefcase: "Grace."

"Who's Grace?" he'd asked, gesturing toward the tag.

"Oh, God's grace," replied Smyth.

"God is named Grace?"

"No. I thought you asked, 'Whose grace?'"

"I beg your pardon?"

"I mean, it's the grace of God—that's whose grace it is. The label on my bag—that's the name of a magazine, a church magazine. *Grace*. I'm the editor."

"Oh," Prestwyck had said, and that was when the atmosphere had changed. Was Smyth being pigeonholed, dismissed as a religious fanatic or a harmless fool? Or was the officer responding badly to the "Who's on first?" routine.

"What's your real name?" Prestwyck had continued.

"I told you. Smyth, John Smyth—like S-m-i-t-h, only with a *Y* instead of an *I*."

"Why?"

"That's right. *Y*."

"No, *why*. Why do you spell your name with a *Y*?"

"Well, just family tradition. My parents and grandparents spelled it that way. Probably due to some spelling error in a wedding register or something. They were English peasants. Not my parents, my more distant ancestors. You see, there wasn't a dictionary in English until Dr. Johnson in the eighteenth century. It was oral—the language. Any spelling was acceptable as long as it was close to what the word sounded like."

Smyth had known he was babbling, but he couldn't seem to stop. He'd had to show Prestwyck his driver's license before he was believed.

He didn't really blame the policeman for being skeptical. John Smith did sound like an assumed name—sometimes even to John Smyth.

Sergeant Robert Prestwyck did not normally work at the airport. He had happened to be there on another matter. Upon learning of John Smyth's approach to the other RCMP officer, however, he had taken charge of the case as the senior officer on site.

Technically, a murder committed in the city of Winnipeg fell within the jurisdiction of the city police, while the RCMP policed the surrounding province of Manitoba. However, as Prestwyck explained to city police detective Alexander Devorkian that evening, "We don't know for sure *where* he saw the murder, so we don't know for sure it was in the city."

Devorkian was about to retort, "Where else would there be a subdivision?" There were only one or two tiny urban areas outside the city limits, and planes usually didn't fly over them. But he knew he could not precisely pinpoint the location of the supposed crime either.

One of the reasons Devorkian was not pressing the matter was that he was not convinced there had been a murder. Apparently the witness was some sort of religious type, and Devorkian did not trust religious people. He never had, not since his childhood in a Ukrainian Orthodox church in North Winnipeg, listening to a vaguely senile priest who blathered on about love but never seemed to notice that the Devorkian children came to church with holes in their shoes and bruises on their faces, both gifts of an alcoholic father. If the only evidence for the "murder" was the "eyewitness account" of some delusional religious nut, he was just as happy to leave the case in the hands of the RCMP.

The taxi wove through narrow side streets toward the heart of the city. The youngish driver maneuvered between the parked cars as skillfully as generations of his ancestors had threaded bicycle carts through the meandering streets of Calcutta. His English was not very good yet. Smyth normally tried to talk to these drivers anyway—most of the taxi drivers in Winnipeg were Indo-Canadians these days—but this time he was glad to sit in silence. He needed time to think, or ponder, or—if the issue in question had been a Bible verse, he would have called it meditating. But it was not a Bible verse, just a strange image that lurked in his mind and would not go away.

The taxi pulled up before a stucco, story-and-a-half house on a narrow street lined with older cars and spreading elm trees. A white picket fence surrounded the yard. That had almost been a mistake. Painting every one of those pickets—three coats to withstand the prairie winter—had taken forever. But the fence was worth it. It made the gray stucco house inviting, proclaiming that a family lived there instead of a shifting collection of boarders who had no roots, no future, and no hope.

The house had had some of the windows replaced. A large picture window flooded the small living room with light. The floors tilted slightly from sitting too long on the deep black prairie gumbo. But the foundation was solid, having survived at least two or three floods when the Red River had overflowed.

As the taxi driver was handing him his suitcase from the trunk, Smyth saw his wife standing in the doorway. Ruby was a petite, energetic woman with flaming red hair—the reason her parents had named her Ruby. She disliked the name Ruby Smyth because it sounded so inelegant, but he had often reminded her gently that it would have been worse if her hair had been black and her parents had named her for that: "After all, it would sound kind of strange if I said I were married to a Black Smith."

Three children aged five to nine raced down the sidewalk to meet him and wrapped themselves around his arms and legs. The Smyths had been granted that rare privilege of having all the children they'd originally wanted—two boys and two girls, Michael, Matthew, Elizabeth, and Anne. Michael, too old at eleven to be seen hugging his father in public, stood behind Ruby on the doorstep. Ruby embraced John warmly as he struggled up the front steps. "Where have you been?" she demanded in his ear. "I was worried. The plane landed hours ago." A slight exaggeration.

Ah, he thought with a smile. *Now the real interrogation begins.*

"So you've got yourself a witness from the heavens?" Devorkian's tone was skeptical, almost condescending.

Prestwyck nodded, accepting the technical meaning of the question, even if he was not happy with its tone.

Detective Devorkian was a tall, gray-haired man who had the knack of looking more military and straight-backed in his gray civilian suit than Prestwyck did in his blue-and-tan RCMP uniform—and a habitual curl of his upper lip made it clear he was aware of the difference.

"A religious man, is he? Saw a murder from an airplane? Did he see an angel on the wing too?"

"Actually, he seemed a pretty reliable witness. Just said what he'd seen, didn't make it flow like a story, didn't try to fill in the details he didn't know."

"You mean you think he really did see a murder?"

"Well, the plane must have been still a couple of thousand feet up, or at least quite a few hundred. And the plane was moving. Said he was staring out the window, just looking, not really paying that much attention. Then he saw it, whatever it was. I'm sure he saw something, but whether it was a murder I don't know. I don't think he's really sure, either—which is another reason I think he's a fairly credible witness."

Devorkian pursed his lips, lowered his eyebrows, tilted his head, and squinted at the sergeant. "So the most credible witnesses are the ones who don't know what they're talking about?"

Prestwyck shrugged. Devorkian would have made him uncomfortable even if relations between the city police and the RCMP weren't habitually strained. "They're less likely to exaggerate," he offered.

"But he's one of those holy-roller types, right? Inclined to see visions, always looking for evil behind every shrub."

"Oh, I don't think that's really it. It's more . . ."

Devorkian's eyes widened slightly, and his eyebrows inched up. "It's more what?"

"Well, you'd have to have seen him."

"Seen him?"

"Yeah, he's short—about five, five one—bald, a little pudgy, with a full gray-and-red beard and little wire-rimmed glasses."

"So?"

"All the time I was taking his statement, I kept thinking he looked like one of the seven dwarfs. I swear at any time I expected him to throw a toy shovel over his shoulder and march out singing, 'Heigh-ho, heigh-ho; it's off to work we go.'"

"Well, if we find Snow White dead somewhere—in a backyard—we'll at least know who did it. We'll put out an APB for the wicked queen."

Prestwyck shrugged again. "There may be something to his story, but I wouldn't know where you should start looking. His description would cover half the houses in Winnipeg. And the plane made a couple of circles over the city before landing."

"So you checked the flight path," Devorkian interrupted. "You do believe him."

"Not necessarily, but I thought it couldn't hurt to check. It actually passed over a lot of the city. The house he saw could be anywhere."

"In any case," Devorkian said, "if someone is dead, we'll know soon enough."

Jul

Sunday	Monday	Tuesday	Wec
	1 Canada Day	2	3
7	8	9	10

Chapter 2

MONDAY, JUNE 17

"No!"

"But it's true, sir. The board has appointed Jim Bakker to be your coeditor. It has asked Jimmy Swaggart to write a series of articles on integrity. It has agreed to publish a swimsuit edition featuring Tammy Faye. . . ."

The conversation was interrupted by a loud ringing of the alarm clock. Smyth sat up in a cold sweat. Ruby still slept peacefully beside him in the bed.

I sure hope I was dreaming, he thought, numbly reaching for the alarm. *I must have been. Rachel never calls me sir.*

Smyth went into work a half-hour late on Monday. The hard part about going to weekend conferences, he reflected, was the extra work. Being away on Friday and maybe even Thursday would put him a day or two behind in his regular work. Writing a report of the conference would cost him an extra couple of days' work. He could not afford to take off Monday to make up for working the weekend, though he did allow himself the luxury of a leisurely breakfast with his family—or as leisurely as was possible with four kids trying to tell him about their weekend. A happy breakfast, at any rate.

The denominational headquarters of the Grace Evangelical Church of North America occupied a squat, crowded, two-story building on a major street near the edge of the inner city, about five blocks from John Smyth's house. It had been at this location on Clifford Street ever since the denomination's beginning during an evangelical revival in the late nineteenth century.

Smyth strolled casually into the office, or as casually as one can while burdened with two overstuffed briefcases of reports and an old brown camera bag. At the secretary's desk outside his office sat the real Rachel—blonde, beautiful, cheerful, efficient, and happily married to a devoted husband named Kurt Woods.

Smyth smiled at Rachel, said "Good morning," and passed into his office.

Sitting down at his cluttered desk, he glanced through the additions that had been made to the clutter in his absence.

"Exceeding wondrous blessings are striking us, the little flock in Minneapolis, like bolts of lightning out of the blue heaven . . ."

John Smyth sighed. Another church report that would need a lot of editing. Oh, he had no doubt that God *was* blessing the little flock. But the report was written in such florid language it would *seem* unbelievable. The "little flock," for instance, was a medium-sized congregation of around 350 people.

"Our new Grace to Face program," the report continued, "has changed the face of our church." The report went on to describe commitments the church members had made to be friends to people outside the church. It then told three stories, complete with photos, to demonstrate how the program was working.

"At eighteen, Dan thought there was no purpose in living —until Pete, a Grace Church member, met him in a hospital ward." The story went on for several paragraphs, describing Dan's difficult childhood, his drug overdose, and his eventual conversion to Christian faith.

"Moira was a very troubled woman when she came to a Bible study at Shirley's house," another story began. "At the end of that first session, she stayed behind and begged Shirley to pray with her. Ten minutes later, Shirley had led her to commit her life to Jesus Christ, and she was filled with joy."

That was all. Not much of a story there. Smyth sighed again. He knew he would have to phone for more details. Later, maybe, when he was a little less distracted.

Was she really dead? Smyth wondered. The woman he had seen from the plane, not the woman in the story.

The third story was better—about a man who had left the church eighteen years before, when his wife had died, and now had returned to faith. Like the first story, it went on for several paragraphs.

Smyth rubbed his tired eyes, and for the tenth time his mind wandered. Had he really seen what he seemed to have seen? Had a woman really been shot? Had Smyth read so many "exceeding wondrous" stories that he was starting to imagine stories that were not there? He was probably more tired from the trip than he cared to admit.

After a coffee break with the other staff and another hour of staring at words on paper, Smyth sighed again and pushed the editing away. He was having trouble concentrating. Perhaps he should try something else. He pulled the phone toward him and made five phone calls before lunch.

Smyth's first phone call was to Tom Ferris, a pastor in Saskatchewan. The conversation would be easy, because he and Tom were old friends. In fact, Smyth shared that kind of relationship with many of the pastors in the denomination—a natural consequence of many years working together and talking over coffee at conferences.

"Hi, Tom. How are you doing? I heard you resigned as pastor of your congregation, and I wanted to get the details for the magazine."

"How did you know about this? I only resigned last night!"

"John Evans, the denominational minister in Vancouver, heard it from Jose Pondero in California this morning, he told Jake Pendanz in this office, and Jake told me at coffee break."

"If it's already known in Vancouver and California, why bother to publish it at all?"

"All right, all right. I know the magazine is only the second fastest means of communication in the denomination. We don't even try to compete with the grapevine for speed—but sometimes we like to think we are more accurate."

"Does that mean you will print the real reason for my resignation?" Ferris asked mischievously.

"Sure, if you can explain it clearly in one paragraph."

Smyth's second call was to a writer in Toronto whose commissioned article was three days overdue. A cheerful voice on the answering machine encouraged Smyth to leave a message and promised that the writer would get back to him promptly. Smyth left the message, but he didn't take the promise very seriously.

A cheerful secretary answered his third call, to Minneapolis.

"Hi. It's John Smyth. Could I talk to Carl Brager please? . . . Carl? . . . Good to talk to you. It's John Smyth."

"John, you usually only phone pastors when they resign. I haven't resigned, have I? You'd think I would remember."

"No, no, Carl. It's this report on the Grace to Face program. Sounds pretty exciting."

"Yeah, it's going really well. We're happy about it. People's lives are really being changed."

"The thing is, Carl . . . the story about Moira—well, it seems rather short."

"Oh, that. Well, the truth is, there's not much more to tell. This woman, Moira Campani, came to the Bible study. She'd heard about it from one of our regulars—met her in a checkout line at the grocery store. She came; she seemed moved by the study and very serious. It was like she had heard the gospel before and was ready to accept it but knew it would cost her. Something to do with her husband. He was involved in drug dealing or something, and Shirley got the impression he had a violent temper. Moira said she would have to confront him, and she wasn't sure how he would take it. I don't know exactly what she was going to confront him with; maybe she just meant she was going to tell him about Jesus. Anyway, Moira became a committed Christian, and she seemed very happy about it. Said she was glad to become part of God's family because she said she'd never had any real friends or family. Shirley was sure the conversion was genuine. But Moira had just recently moved to Minneapolis and was going to move away again right away—in fact, I think she's already gone. About all Shirley could do was give Moira a Grace to Face pendant, pray for her, and let God take care of the rest."

"That's it? No forwarding address or anything?"

"Not as far as I know. Shirley said she just stopped coming

to the Bible study, and she hadn't wanted to give out her phone number."

"Thanks, Carl. It's actually an interesting story, but I don't think we can print it. I mean, if she's already gone, we can't do any follow-up, can't verify any of this. We have to be careful to publish only what we know is true."

"Sure, John. I understand. It would be fine to just do the other two stories."

"Okay. Say hi to Shirley for me."

His fourth call was to Clint Granowski, a pastor who was starting a new church in southwest Winnipeg.

"Clint Granowski." A cheerful voice responded to his call. "Good morning!"

"Clint, it's John Smyth. I understand you called while I was gone."

"Oh, great, John! It's good to hear your voice! How are you?!"

Smyth smiled. He had observed before that church planters—pastors starting new churches—tended to be enthusiastic people.

"Good, Clint. Did you want something in particular?"

"Yeah, we're having our first baptism Sunday afternoon, and we wanted to invite you to come. We've got three people being baptized!"

"Great, Clint. Where are you going to have it?" The new congregation was only a few months old and didn't have a building yet. Its Sunday services were being held in a school.

"In the Collinsons' swimming pool, 425 Mapleleaf. That's our street, but a few blocks down. Do you know the Collinsons? They're great people, really on fire for the Lord, wonderful people. They've got this big pool and a big yard. Can you come?"

"I'd love to, Clint. What time?"

"Two-thirty."

"Great, Clint. See you then."

Something else to do on a weekend, Smyth thought. But he knew he wanted to attend the baptism. He never tired of hearing how people had come to faith in Christ and seeing them welcomed into the Christian family.

Smyth dialed a fifth number.

"I'd like to speak to Sergeant Prestwyck, please."

An officious voice responded, "I'm not sure if he is available. Whom shall I say is calling?"

"John Smyth."

There was a pause. "Please hold."

After about a minute, a low, breathless voice said, "Sergeant Prestwyck."

"Hi. This is John Smyth."

"Okay." The voice sounded tense and noncommittal. "You want to tell me something?"

"No. I mean, this really is John Smyth."

"Okay . . . Oh. You mean, the religious writer." The voice dripped disappointment.

"Uh . . . yeah." Normally Smyth would have taken issue with the term "religious writer"—he saw himself as committed specifically to Christianity, not to religion in general—but this time he let it pass.

"Look, I need to make this quick," Sergeant Prestwyck was saying. "They called me out of an interrogation to answer the phone. Thought it might be . . . never mind. Did you remember something else?"

"No," Smyth hesitated. "I was just wondering if you had . . . uh . . . found a body."

A loud sigh. “No, we haven’t found a body. If we do, believe me, we’ll let you know.”

There was a loud click and a hum.

Chapter 3

SUNDAY, JUNE 23

The afternoon sun shone brightly from the blue prairie sky as John and Ruby Smyth drove down Mapleleaf Street on Sunday. Parked cars lined both sides of the street. Smyth found a spot about a block away from number 425 and pulled their old, gray station wagon in to the curb.

Following the sidewalk around the side of the house and through a gate, they found themselves in a good-sized backyard. About sixty people were sitting in lawn chairs or standing chatting by a swimming pool. The water sparkled in the sunshine.

Near the gate, a blonde woman was talking animatedly to an older, gray-haired woman, her head bobbing enthusiastically to emphasize her words.

". . . then suddenly this head came over the fence. I didn't see it at first, and then it said hello. It was a woman, and she looked so funny—just a head with short black hair sitting on the fence. I laughed and then I apologized, and she laughed too. She said she was the new neighbor and had just come to join her husband. The house was empty for several months, you know, and then a week or so ago we thought we saw a man there, and Clint talked to him once and he just said his name was Randy or something. He just kind of brushed Clint off, but we were still hoping we could get to know him. I mean, maybe he was just in a hurry that day, or maybe he is mean and unhappy, but that just means he needs the Lord more, right? Anyway, we had never seen his wife before, but she said she had just come, and we talked a little, and she seemed very friendly and happy, but a bit nervous, you know. So I just asked her right out, 'Do you love Jesus?' And she said, 'Yes!' She was hoping to find evangelical Christians here, and she was just amazed how the Lord answered her prayer the first moment she arrived. She was waiting for her husband to come home. She seemed a bit worried about him, said he wasn't a Christian yet, and I said maybe we could lead him to love Jesus, but I had to leave right then. Anyway, I said Clint would be home in five or ten minutes, so I left her. I was going to invite her to the baptism, but she wasn't home today."

She paused for a second, and Ruby opened her mouth to say hello. Then she closed it as the blonde woman started up again. Ruby smiled at John and cocked an amused eyebrow. Carol Granowski could go on for hours, it seemed, and never come up for air.

"Oh, but there's this other couple who just moved in down the street a couple of months ago, a retired couple named John and Liz Freeman—we invited them. And Gary and Grace Drummond—you know they've really struggled in their marriage, and if they would only learn to love Jesus, I'm sure things would be a lot better, but you know sometimes people just seem to want to do things the hard way. Maybe things would be different if they could only have children. I hope she hasn't left him again. I tried to phone her a couple of times this week to invite her over for coffee, but she wasn't there, and Gary sounded rather evasive. Anyway, Clint invited Gary to come today, but he wouldn't say if he would come, and there are John and Ruby. Hi!"

Now Carol flashed an enormous smile, wagged her head, and came bouncing over to the Smyths, throwing her arms around Ruby in a welcoming hug. John just stood there smiling, enjoying her energy. Carol and her husband, Clint, were cheerful, effervescent people who saw hopeful possibilities in every dark stranger, and their energy was infectious. John Smyth liked them for it. Such faith and hope were at the heart of their Christianity—the belief that God could, and frequently did, turn sinners into saints.

The afternoon progressed with lively conversation and quite a few more hugs. The group gathered to sing a few gospel songs with guitar accompaniment, then circled the pool for the baptisms. The three candidates—a middle-aged husband and wife and a teenaged boy—stood with Clint in the waist-deep water at the shallow end of the pool. One by one, they told the story of how they came to love Jesus. Then Clint dipped each one backward into the water and brought him or her up again, drenched and radiant.

John Smyth enjoyed the event, as he always did, but he had trouble keeping his mind on what was being said and done. Part of him still seemed to be walking in a dream, a dream that had begun with a view from an airplane and would end, if at all, only when a cold body was found in some backyard.

The last rays of the setting sun had stolen silently out of the Drummond house a half-hour earlier, yet no lights had been turned on. A man sat wordlessly on the sofa, staring into the darkness, yet not seeing it. The darkness in the house seemed bright to him in comparison with the darkness in his heart. He was only numbly aware of the depths of that darkness, and if he could have articulated it at all, he would probably have said only that Grace had gone out of his life.

That was true, and yet perhaps it wasn't. He knew his wife was not coming back, but in another sense he could feel her still with him, staring at him, accusing him. As disturbed as he was about her absence, in another sense he feared she would always be with him, haunting his existence as long as he lived.

Gary Drummond got up at last and shuffled toward the kitchen. As he passed by the phone, he paused. He toyed with the idea of phoning her family in Alberta again, pretending to be looking for her. He didn't. It was useless. He knew she wasn't there. Besides, he was tired now. He didn't even have the strength to keep up the pretense, to maintain the facade of a loving husband. He moved on toward the beer in the refrigerator, seeking another form of darkness—the darkness of oblivion.

Chapter 4

MONDAY, JUNE 24

The clink of the mail slot and the plop of letters on the floor echoed around Apartment 307 on the third floor of the Livingstone Apartments, causing no ripple on the dust that had been collecting on every flat surface for over a week. By the time the echo had died in the midmorning silence, the mail carrier had already moved swiftly down the corridor to disturb the silence in the next empty apartment.

Later, in the soft early evening, David Mackenzie shuffled down Main Street. It was like every other Main Street in the old downtown core in every other Canadian city. It had a number of monuments to urban renewal—city hall, the provincial museum, the luxurious Centennial Auditorium, and several bank towers on the windiest corner in Canada. But none of these, collectively or individually, could save Main Street from itself. It was a shabby street fronted by boarded-up buildings, pawnshops, a mission storefront or two, and a row of seedy bars and hotels that catered to drunks and prostitutes. Soggy cardboard, cigarette butts, and discarded cups from fast-food restaurants littered the sidewalk. The street with its buildings was one of the few in Winnipeg that seemed permanently stained with black soot and grime —and with no major industry to excuse it. Perhaps it lingered there from long-past CPR locomotives or seeped out under the doors from the filthy life within.

Winnipeg had thirty murders a year, twenty-five of them in knife fights between alcoholics in Main Street bars. David should know—he was one of the alcoholics. He shuffled further down the street, looking around him with a puzzled stare. He was looking for Grace.

She was not here. She had not been here for a week. Not that she kept office hours—hookers never did—but he would have seen her if she'd been around. Hookers had habits. They also had enemies, mostly bad tricks. David was worried.

He shuffled along further, eyes darting here and there. But David's eyes always did that, whether he was looking for anyone or anything or not.

David had no friends. Grace was not his friend either. But she had talked to him a few times. And he had admired her. For the last three months he had admired her almost every day. And now she was gone.

Chapter 5

MONDAY, JULY 1

East of Winnipeg, the Trans-Canada Highway rolls on across the flat prairie, bounded on both sides by wheat fields. Halfway to the Ontario border, without any change in the flatness of the land, the fields suddenly give way to scrub woods—a vast sea of spindly stalks, twenty to thirty feet tall, gray, uninteresting, and commercially marginal. Here, at the edge of the woods and half an hour from the city, stretched the Goerzen farm, 1,320 acres of black gumbo and golden wheat.

On this Monday afternoon, the sun shone down relentlessly from a cloudless blue sky. Duane Goerzen, seventeen years old, tall, blond, and muscular, whistled for the family dog and walked lazily toward the cool of the woods at the edge of the farm. Even there, the relentless sun poked through the gray and green branches, mottling the dark, brown floor of the woods with bright splotches.

Duane and the dog pushed through the undergrowth,

enjoying the afternoon. A slight breeze stirred the leaves, and a flicker of piercing brightness caught Duane's eye. About the same time, old Sam, who had bounded on ahead, shied away, jumping sideways and baying a long, frightful howl.

Duane hurried forward. He stopped suddenly, arrested first by her nakedness, and blushed in surprise and embarrassment. His eyes brushed slowly upward toward her face, where they stopped again, and he stared openmouthed, embarrassment giving way to shock. He knew then that she was dead.

Prairie farmers often work late in August, harvesting their wheat by searchlights mounted on their combines long after the late evening sun has retired for the night. That July evening the RCMP worked the same hours, keeping watch over the piece of ground where they had gathered a harvest of clues among gray stalks of tree trunks.

Prestwyck arrived late on the scene, as the forensics people were finishing their work and the last light was fading from the sky. This area was not his usual beat, but when he had learned of the discovery, he had decided to make use of the privileges of his senior rank.

One of the advantages of doing police work on the prairies was the relative isolation. Prestwyck brushed past the only two reporters who had learned of Duane Goerzen's discovery.

"Sergeant," one of them called, "what's going on here?"

Prestwyck paused and half turned back. He looked the reporter over. He knew Scott Ledyear slightly as a reporter for the *Winnipeg New Times,* although he couldn't bring to mind anything Ledyear had written. He hesitated a few seconds before replying, "A body has been found in these woods. We don't yet know who it is or how the person died."

"Is it a man or a woman?" asked Ledyear.

"We're not ready to release that information," Prestwyck said. He could tell from Ledyear's face that the reporter already knew it was a woman. "We'll have a press conference at ten in the morning." He turned on his heel and walked into the woods.

Night settled slowly on southern Manitoba, the air remaining hot and oppressive even though the sun had gone down. It was too hot and sticky to sleep well, and many Winnipeggers tossed fitfully in their beds—among them John Smyth, Gary Drummond, and Alexander Devorkian. David Mackenzie, stretched out on a piece of cardboard on cool cement behind a large garbage bin, for once slept better than any of them.

Chapter 6

TUESDAY, JULY 2

By eight the next morning, Sergeant Prestwyck was sitting at his meticulously arranged desk at Division D headquarters on Portage Avenue in Winnipeg, glancing over the preliminary forensics report. On the other side of the desk sat Leo Lazinski, head of the forensics team. He had been up all night, and he looked haggard.

"All right," Prestwyck said. "Give me the basics and then go home. I'll read the rest later."

Lazinski shrugged. "A white female, black hair, five-foot-four, one hundred thirty-five pounds, age perhaps midtwenties."

"How long had she been there?"

"Couple of weeks, perhaps."

Prestwyck hesitated a moment, but Lazinski, stifling a yawn, failed to notice. It had been two weeks since Prestwyck had met John Smyth. "What did she die of?"

"Don't know. Too early to tell." Then, seeing Prestwyck's

look, Lazinski added, "Could've been the bullet that tore out the front of her mouth and half of her brain."

Prestwyck paused again. "Yeah," he said dryly, "could've been that."

"Well, she could have been poisoned, for instance, and shot afterward."

"Why?"

"To make her harder to identify."

"Is the face recognizable?"

"Part of it, but the bullet did a fair amount of damage, plus it looks as if some kind of small animal may have nibbled at the face after she was shot. The mess would confuse any witness who looked at it."

"So, if we need to release a picture of her, we'd have to rely on an artist's drawing?"

"Most likely."

"Will we have to?" He turned toward a balding, forty-year-old man in a rumpled RCMP uniform, who had just come in the door. "Have you identified her, Osnachuck?"

"No," the man in the doorway replied. "There was no ID, of course, and we haven't been able to connect her to any missing-persons report."

"Better get the artist in then. Go on, Lazinski."

"There were no other marks on the body, other than a few bruises and scratches."

"Bruises and scratches?"

"Nothing very significant. Most people have some. Most of hers might not have been connected to the murder at all, but some of the scratches appear to have happened after she died, perhaps when she was moved."

"She was moved?"

"Probably. We can tell by the pooling of blood in the body. Also, there's not a lot of blood at the site, considering, and it didn't look like it had rained since she was dumped there. Some of the teeth and facial bones are missing."

"When did it rain last? Osnachuck, do you know?"

The man by the door shrugged. "I don't think for two or three weeks."

"I don't *think* so either, Osnachuck. Find out." Turning back to Lazinski, Prestwyck said, "Did you search the ground for the teeth?"

"Pretty well, but we'll do a more thorough search of the whole area today. Nothing so far."

"What about the scratches?"

"Those may be connected. Some look like fingernail marks, perhaps when the killer ripped her clothes off." Anticipating the next question, he continued, "We think the clothes were ripped off because we found fragments of white cloth by the body."

"*White* cloth?"

"Yes, some from her underwear, but also some that looks like dress material."

"So the clothes were ripped off at the scene?"

"Looks like—some of them, anyway."

"And that was after she was dead? So she wasn't raped or sexually assaulted?"

"No evidence of it. Won't know for sure until the medical examination."

"Then why rip her clothes off?"

"To make it harder to identify her?"

"So we have no ID, no clothes, and half the teeth are missing. Are there enough teeth left to identify her?"

"Maybe not conclusively, but enough to help. We could at least eliminate some possibilities."

"How about fingerprints?"

"Some decomposition, but we got some passable prints."

"So, the killer takes her clothes and her teeth, but leaves her fingers intact. That means her fingerprints aren't on file, and the killer knew it."

"That or he isn't too bright."

"Yeah. He should know we can get prints from her house or apartment."

"Or car. It might have been someone passing through on the Trans-Canada."

Prestwyck paused. That was a good probability. Why, he wondered, had he been assuming the woman was local, from a Winnipeg suburb? White clothes. It had been two weeks. He shook himself out of his reverie. "So what we really have at this point is nothing—and there's a press conference scheduled for ten. It'll probably be some time before we even have a name."

"Grace."

"What?"

"Grace," Lazinski repeated. "Her name is Grace."

This time there was a long pause. Prestwyck stared at Lazinski. "Her name is Grace? How do you know? Have you been holding out on me?"

"We found a necklace on the body, a long chain with the word 'Grace' hanging on it."

"You're saying the killer shoots out her dental work, rips off her clothes so she won't be identified, then leaves a name tag hanging around her neck?!"

"Maybe he didn't know it was there. It was a long chain, could have hung down inside the clothes. If he ripped the clothes off there in the dark, he might not have noticed it."

"In the dark. Now you know it was in the dark. What else do you know?"

"Well, it makes sense. If I were dumping a body, I'd do it at night. He missed the pieces of cloth, remember."

"Any other jewelry?"

"No. Some ring indentations on her fingers."

"Wedding ring?"

"Can't tell from the indentations."

"On the wedding ring *finger?*"

"Yeah. Possibly two rings."

Prestwyck sighed. "So she may have been married. Anything else?"

"No. Some signs of foot traffic but no clear prints. It hasn't rained in . . . well, in a while. The highway's a couple of hundred feet away."

"I know where the highway is!" Prestwyck snapped.

"Some leaves thrown over the body, not really buried. It was probably done in a hurry."

"So it means he didn't care if the body was found eventually, just wanted to delay us finding it. Okay, Lazinski, anything else?"

"Not yet. I'll let you know when we find something. Autopsy's scheduled for later today."

"Okay, go home and get some rest."

Constable Bisset stuck her head in the doorway. "Detective Devorkian from the Winnipeg Police Department is on line three."

Prestwyck hesitated.

Bisset continued. "I told him you were in a conference, and he said he would hold. I told him it was going to be a long conference, and he said he would still hold . . ."

"Okay, I get the idea," Prestwyck said. He already had two messages from Devorkian on his desk. "Tell Corporal Gillespie to come in. I need to brief her before the press conference."

"I can't do that, sir. She just phoned in sick. She has the flu."

"Okay, I'll take the press conference myself." Prestwyck was not really upset at the development. He may not have had Gillespie's rapport with the press, but this way he could control things better. They would have to be careful what they said at the press conference—especially with Devorkian poking around.

Prestwyck waited a few moments before picking up the phone. "Devorkian. What can I do for you?" He didn't try to fake enthusiasm.

"Prestwyck, what are you doing, holding out on me?"

"Holding out? What are you talking about?"

"Come on, Prestwyck, the body you found. Don't tell me you weren't going to tell me about it."

"Well, sure. When we get to the point where we are looking for someone or want some help, we'll circulate a bulletin."

"Circulate a bulletin, my Aunt Fanny! Is this the woman that religious guy saw from the plane or not? If it is, it's my jurisdiction, and I want it!"

"I thought you weren't interested. Back off, Devorkian. This body is ours, found fifty kilometers from Winnipeg. Off the Trans-Canada. Probably just somebody passing through. She could be from any city in Canada."

"So it is a woman?"

Prestwyck paused. "That doesn't mean anything. If you find a body, the odds are fifty-fifty it will be a woman."

"Some women's groups might say closer to ninety-five to five."

"Very funny." Prestwyck was thawing a little. "Okay, it was a woman, and it could have been the woman Mr. Smyth saw, but we don't know. We don't even know he *saw* a woman. There's no evidence to link her."

"What do you mean, no evidence? When did she die?"

"Two weeks ago."

Devorkian snorted. "So there you are."

"So . . . nothing."

"What was she wearing?"

"Nothing." Prestwyck was pleased with that answer.

"What *had* she been wearing?"

Prestwyck sighed. "We're not sure. Probably something white. Look, we'll cooperate on this. There could be a connection. We don't know. Come over and we'll give you a copy of the file."

"Why don't you bring it to me?"

"Don't push it."

The press conference, held at RCMP headquarters, was a major affair by Winnipeg standards: eight or nine radio and TV people, reporters and photographers from the city's two main newspapers, and—coming in just after they started and standing at the back—Detective Devorkian from the Winnipeg Police.

Prestwyck began by reading a short statement. A woman, Caucasian, short black hair, probably in her twenties, had been found in a woods about fifty kilometers east of Winnipeg, just off the Trans-Canada Highway. The body had been there for some time. Police suspected foul play. Her identity was unknown.

Then the questions began. Was the woman fully dressed?

The police would rather not say more until the victim's family had been notified. The reporters wrote that down as a no.

Had she been sexually assaulted?

Police didn't know yet.

How long was "some time"? That was Ledyear's question.

Prestwyck thought about it. Probably between a week and a month—the medical examination was not complete.

The fencing continued for some time, with Prestwyck giving away little new information.

An hour later, Devorkian dropped the file on the front edge of Prestwyck's desk. Prestwyck was leaning back in the chair behind the desk. Devorkian sat ramrod straight in the other chair, his gray suit wrinkle free. "You were holding out on me," he said.

"Why? There's not much there. We don't know who the woman is or how she died."

"There are two key facts you didn't tell me. Both of them link the woman to your fanatic."

Prestwyck glared at Devorkian. "You mean my *witness*?"

Devorkian shrugged and didn't answer. Finally Prestwyck sighed. "What are the two facts?"

"First, she was shot in the mouth. Your . . . *witness* said her mouth opened wide."

"Right. He said her mouth opened wide, not that it got shot off."

"What would that look like from a couple of thousand feet up?"

"From a couple of thousand feet up, he probably couldn't even see her face."

"Not from a couple of thousand feet up."

"What do you mean?"

Again Devorkian did not answer. Instead he continued, "Fact number two: Her name was Grace."

"So?"

"So what did the nametags on the fan—I mean the witness's—luggage say?"

"They said Grace, but he explained that. It's the name of the magazine he edits."

"Could be it was her luggage."

"Don't be silly."

"Did you check to see that *Grace* magazine really exists?"

"We're working on it," said Prestwyck, making a mental note, knowing that Devorkian noticed.

"Missed that one, eh?"

"Why bother? We didn't believe there really was a murder, did we?"

Devorkian changed topics. "Why didn't you give more information to the press?"

"We don't want to release too many details. That would be a heck of a way for someone to find out their daughter or wife was dead."

That sneer again. "Yeah, it's much kinder to keep the thing a secret and let the family live in uncertainty for a few more weeks."

Prestwyck deliberately leaned farther back, crossed his legs, and raised an eyebrow. "Well, then, why don't you just check out your missing-persons file and tell us who she is?"

"We already have," Devorkian admitted. "Nothing likely."

"So she's not from Winnipeg."

"She still could be."

Prestwyck snorted. "You don't know any more than we do. All we've got is a Jane Doe murdered by a John Doe."

"So now you have them married?"

"Okay, murdered by a John Smith."

"John Smyth with a *Y*, maybe."

"Back to him again? Don't be stupid. John Smyth was two thousand feet up in a plane."

"How do you know? It makes a pretty good alibi. You establish an alibi two thousand feet up in the air, you land, you tell the police, then you go commit murder. Hide the body for two weeks and you're home free. Cops won't be able to determine precise time of death."

"Yeah, great plan. Fools everyone but the Winnipeg Police."

Now Devorkian glared at Prestwyck. He stood and picked up the file. "I'll be in touch," he said and walked out.

Chapter 7

WEDNESDAY, JULY 3

"Police can't identify dead woman" blared Scott Ledyear's headline. It had been a slow news day—he had won a front-page spot for his story, and he was making the most of it.

"Police have confirmed that the body discovered Monday in a woods outside Winnipeg was a woman," ran the article. "They seem to have determined little else—such as who she is, how she died . . ."

Prestwyck crumpled up the paper and threw it onto the floor. He made a note that in the future he would tell Ledyear nothing. If he ever found out anything.

Alexander Devorkian, however, chortled to himself when he read Ledyear's article. Until, that is, he realized the article had not clarified that it was the RCMP who were ignorant and not the city police.

John Smyth did not ordinarily watch TV news. He considered the newspaper a much more reliable source of information.

The drawback was that the *Winnipeg New Times* was a "morning" paper and contained only yesterday's news, even though it was delivered to John Smyth's house after he had gone to work in the morning. By Wednesday afternoon, therefore, Smyth still did not know about the body that had been found.

He walked home through the oppressive afternoon heat and pondered some of the far-reaching choices he had made in his life. Why had he chosen to live in a city with such extremes of temperature? Why did he walk to work anyway? Why had he not bought a new car with air conditioning? While he was asking, why had he not bought a Rolls Royce? Why had he not chosen to be a televangelist instead of a modestly paid, hardworking denominational employee?

There were answers to such questions, of course, good answers. But John was not really looking for answers. The questions were simply something else to think about, a way to keep his mind off the heat and help him make the transition from office to home.

Coming up the sidewalk, he noticed that Ruby was watching from the front window. *It must be something significant,* he thought, *to open the insulating blinds so early in the day.*

Ruby met him at the door and gave him a big hug. Maybe she was just glad to see him. But he knew better.

"What is it?" he asked.

Suddenly serious, she led him into the living room, picked up the newspaper, and handed it to him.

He realized right away, without her pointing it out, which article she wanted him to see. She watched intently while he read Scott Ledyear's entire article.

"Well," she said when he had finished. "Do you think it could be the one you saw?"

"I don't know," he replied quietly. "At this point, looks like it could be anyone."

Gary Drummond wandered aimlessly around his big, empty house, shirtless, his long legs encased in grubby blue jeans. His half-eaten dinner lay cooling on the table. By the time he had gotten home from work, the TV news had been half over, and he had missed the story. He had missed the TV news the night before too, but he had heard some scraps of information that day at work. From the living room through the dining room to the kitchen he walked, then up to the bedrooms and down again. It was as if he was waiting for something. Finally, he pulled on a tee shirt, grabbed a baseball cap from a peg, and walked out the front door, letting it lock behind him.

He strode two blocks down Mapleleaf to a gas station-convenience store. Nonchalantly, he picked up a newspaper and plopped it down on the counter. Scott Ledyear's headline blared up at him.

"Want to check up on the sports," he mumbled to the clerk. Tossing some change on the counter, he picked up the paper and hustled out the door. He walked home faster than he had come.

Reading Scott Ledyear's article, for the first time he began to have doubts. A white woman, short black hair, in her twenties. It was a pretty general description, could fit a lot of women, but still . . .

He was startled by a knock. Looking through the screen door, he saw a medium-sized man standing on the doorstep. His dark hair was silhouetted against the evening sun. His mouth opened in a cheerful grin.

"Hi, Gary," he called. "Mind if I come in?"

"Uh, Pastor Granowski . . . uh, sure."

The man on the doorstep opened the screen door and

stepped inside. "I've told you—call me Clint," he said, smiling up at Drummond, then sat down in a cheap plush chair across from him.

"I haven't seen you around for a while, Gary," Clint Granowski continued. "I was hoping you would come to the baptism a couple of weeks ago."

"Yeah, well, I was kinda busy."

"You mean at work?" Drummond was a mechanic at one of the car dealerships on the west side of the city.

"Naw, not really. Just . . . other stuff. At home. The house. The garden."

"How is work going?"

"Okay. No problems."

"How's Grace?"

There was a long pause this time. Granowski could see she wasn't here. Drummond had to tell him something.

"Has she left again?" Granowski asked gently.

Drummond stretched his jaw tight. "Yeah," he said finally. His jaw worked as if he was going to say more, but he didn't.

"I'm sorry, Gary. When did she leave?"

"About two weeks ago."

"What happened?"

"The usual. We had an argument. She just left."

"Did she go back to her parents in Alberta again?"

Drummond just shrugged.

"Gary, I'd like to help. Perhaps if you'd talk about it, it would help. Carol and I would be glad to talk to the two of you. Carol could phone Grace."

The conversation lurched along for a few more minutes. Drummond squirmed uneasily, but he didn't say much.

Finally Granowski asked, "Would you like to pray about it?"

Granowski prayed. Drummond just sat there.

Standing, Granowski said, "Gary, if you ever feel like talking, if there's anything you think we could do, call me. Carol and I will keep praying for you."

When he was gone, Drummond stared for a long time at the screen door. If only he could actually call him Clint, if he could just get past that formal "Pastor Granowski," perhaps they really could talk. Now, for sure, he needed some "spiritual help." He felt his spirit was dying, shriveling up like a walnut, writhing in pain. Perhaps he could—but it was too late for that. Grace could not come back now. It was too late.

The newspaper had been tossed carelessly on one of the plump, overstuffed chairs in Gladys Plumtre's overcrowded living room, Scott Ledyear's fervid prose staring at the ceiling. Gladys, who could not unfairly be deemed plump and overstuffed herself, was at the door again, talking to yet another tenant.

Her living room was crowded because she had tried to bring as much as possible from her house when she and Fred moved into the Livingstone Apartments as a manager/caretaker couple. She filled it the same way she tried to crowd as much food as possible onto her plate. She was acquisitive by nature.

Though dinner was long past, Gladys still had read only half of Scott Ledyear's article. She loved reading about exciting things like murder, but she had neglected to read the paper that morning, and only when one of the tenants mentioned it had she realized there had been a murder. She had immediately pulled the newspaper out from the pile under the coffee table and begun to read eagerly.

Frustratingly, her reading had been interrupted again and again. It was the day after rent day, since July 1 had been a holiday, and many of the tenants had forgotten to bring their rent checks in on the second, too. Tonight there had been a steady string of tardy tenants, checks in hand, standing at her door.

David Mackenzie reluctantly turned his steps northward on Main Street. Two blocks later, he stopped before a grimy storefront with paint peeling from a sign that said, "Grace Mission."

As David expected, Harry Collins welcomed him at the door. Harry was a short, midfiftyish man, quietly cheerful rather than jovial. He did not live up to his first name—unlike most of the men he served, he was beardless and bald. ("There's no 'ing' in my balding," he would sometimes say in his soft but penetrating voice.) And he was fat rather than round—Main Street required blunt reality.

Harry had come to Grace Mission right out of Bible school to get some experience before becoming a pastor, but he had found his calling and stayed. When old Henry Classen died, Harry Collins had taken over. "The mission is so poor we could afford only initials rather than a full name on the director's office door," Harry liked to explain, "and when Henry died, we couldn't afford to change the initials." It was a joke. There were no letters at all on the director's battered brown door.

Harry had never married. There had never been an opportunity. "I'm married to a girl named Grace Mission," was another one of his standard lines, "and God doesn't allow bigamy."

David didn't especially like Harry Collins—the man preached too much and made David feel guilty because he expected that David could change—but he tolerated Harry for the free meals the mission provided. David preferred food to talk.

Yet it wasn't food David wanted this time. It was information. Harry didn't just talk to the alcoholics who came to the mission. He also went out onto the streets and talked to prostitutes. David would wait until after the meal was served and Harry had given his sermon and then ask to talk to him. Harry might think David wanted to get saved, but David didn't mind. David would ask him about Grace. Perhaps Harry had seen her and knew where she had gone. Or perhaps Harry had talked her into getting saved and getting off the streets. It happened sometimes, people said, but then you never saw the girls again on Main Street.

David had his questions well rehearsed. He had been thinking about them all day. Yet he never asked them because he read the newspaper first.

The mission always stocked newspapers. Harry insisted on it. He believed in reading. If the men could begin to read the newspaper, he always said, maybe they would start reading the Bible too. But David wasn't really interested in the reading. He was just early for supper—without a watch, he had some trouble keeping track of time—and feeling the need for a warm meal before talking to Harry. So he evaded Harry's welcome by picking up the paper. Lost in his thoughts, he looked at the front page without seeing it at first, but something about Scott Ledyear's headline caught his attention. He read the article slowly, twice, sounding it out word for word in an unintelligible mumble.

He was in a daze for most of the meal, thinking about what he had read, unaware of what he was eating. He also heard none of Harry Collins's sermon, though he held his gaze fixed on Harry's face as if he was hanging on every word.

When the sermon was over, he heaved himself to his feet and shuffled toward the door with many of the other men. He would not talk to Harry now. He thought Harry might know what had happened to Grace, but he was not sure, not sure at all that the dead woman was Grace. He needed time to think, time to plan a new bunch of questions. Underneath it all was the street person's habitual reaction to steer clear of trouble. Trouble had a way of breeding more trouble for those who messed with it. Street people carried around too much fear and guilt, and where there was trouble, they understood that they would inevitably be blamed for it. Maybe he would change his mind later, but for now David was playing it safe. He slipped out the door and back onto Main Street.

Chapter 8

THURSDAY, JULY 4

It was eight-thirty on Thursday morning. A female voice answered John Smyth's call on the third ring.

"Could I speak to Sergeant Prestwyck?" John Smyth asked.

"I'm sorry," the voice answered. Smyth heard phones ringing and bustling noises in the background. "Sergeant Prestwyck is not available right now. Can I help you?"

"Uh, no," Smyth replied. "I really want to talk to Sergeant Prestwyck. Do you know where he is? Do you know when he will be available?"

"I'm sorry. I can't tell you that, but perhaps I can reach him. Is it urgent?"

Smyth looked up and saw Rachel standing in the doorway. He hesitated and then said, "Uh, no. It's not urgent. Can you maybe ask him to phone John Smyth?"

"John Smith?"

"Yeah. Tell him it's the religious writer. He has the number."

He looked up at Rachel as he hung up the phone. She raised her eyebrows. "Religious writer?"

"Don't ask. It's a long story."

"There is a policeman here to see you," she said. "A Sergeant Prestwyck of the RCMP."

Smyth jumped involuntarily. He did not respond to the questions in her voice, just nodded silently. He rose as Rachel showed Prestwyck into his cluttered eight-by-ten office.

Prestwyck glanced around, obviously unimpressed. He shut the door before sitting down.

"I was just trying to phone you," Smyth said, feeling he should explain the phone message Prestwyck would receive when he got back to his office.

Prestwyck arched an eyebrow. "Wanting to confess?"

"Uh, no. We don't do that. We're not Catholics."

It was a spur-of-the-moment attempt at humor, given without thinking, but bold nonetheless, Smyth reflected.

Prestwyck actually smiled. "What did you want?" he asked.

"Well, I, uh, read the story in the paper, about the dead woman that was found. I was wondering if she might have been the one that I saw? I mean . . ." His voice trailed off. Smyth realized that even though he had planned what to say to Prestwyck, he had lost control of the conversation already.

"What do you think?" Prestwyck replied. "Do you think it could be?"

"I don't know."

"What did she look like, the woman you saw?"

"I didn't exactly see her face. She had dark hair—short, dark hair, I think."

"How tall was she?"

"I don't know. I was looking down at her. Average, I guess. I didn't notice anything unusual."

"Do you think you would recognize a picture of her?"

"I don't know. I didn't see any details. But I might be able to tell you if it wasn't her."

"Okay. We'll show you a picture later. What was she wearing?"

"I told you that. White. She was wearing a white dress or a white skirt and blouse or a white skirt and sweater."

"A sweater—in June?"

"I don't know. Like I said, I just saw white."

"Could it have been white pants?"

"Maybe. I don't think so."

"You said her mouth opened very wide. What was it like? Was she calling? Or screaming? Singing? Laughing?"

"It was just an impression, that her mouth opened really wide—like an O. I didn't really get the feeling that she was screaming. . . . Maybe it was just that I couldn't hear anything. . . . Maybe she was laughing. Her head jerked a little . . . I don't know. I was a few hundred feet up, you know."

"A few hundred or a few thousand?"

"Several hundred at least. Maybe a couple of thousand. I don't know. It was hard to judge." Smyth felt he was on the verge of babbling again.

Prestwyck paused. When Smyth said nothing more, he asked, "Do you remember anything else?"

Smyth thought a minute. "No."

"Anything at all?"

"No."

"Is this *Grace?*"

Smyth hesitated. "Oh, the magazine. Yes, that's our latest issue."

"May I have a copy?"

"Sure. You can have that one."

"Do you have business cards?"

"Sure." Smyth opened a desk drawer and fumbled around until he found a crumpled card. He smoothed it out and handed it to Prestwyck, who leaned back in his chair.

"Do you like your job, Mr. Smyth?"

"Yes. It's very . . . fulfilling."

"Do you travel much?"

"A little. Maybe once every month or two."

"Where do you go?"

"Conventions, conferences. I visit churches. I research stories."

"How many churches? Where are they?"

"There are about five hundred in our denomination. They're all over North America . . . well, mainly the Midwest and West, out to B.C. and California, not many in Ontario or the eastern U.S."

"Do you meet many women on your travels?"

"Some. I meet—what do you mean?"

"Ever have an affair with one?"

"No! I'm happily married."

"And want to stay that way?"

"Of course."

"So if one of them showed up here in Winnipeg, you would want to keep her from talking."

"Yes . . . no . . . I'm not having an affair. I haven't had any affairs."

"Your job *and* your marriage would depend on you staying away from anything immoral, eh?"

"Yes, but I haven't done anything like . . . like . . ."

Prestwyck was casually flipping through the magazine, seemingly unaware of Smyth's growing discomfort. "So," he said, "who's Grace?"

Smyth blinked. "It's . . . it's the magazine. It's our church.

It's not named after a woman. It's . . . they're named after God's goodness."

"Do you know any women named Grace?"

"Uh . . . a few. I've got an aunt in Ontario. There's a pastor's wife in California. . . . Oh, we've got a writer named Grace in Saskatchewan."

"Any others? Can you write down their names and addresses?"

Smyth nodded his head and pulled a piece of paper from a box under his desk. The paper had writing on the back. Smyth saved old news releases for scrap paper because it saved the church money. He began writing. Eventually he came up with five names, checking addresses in a card file on his desk. "I don't have all the addresses here. But—"

"You can phone them in tomorrow. Is there anything else you would like to say?"

"Uh . . . no. I guess not."

"If you think of anything else, you *will* let us know, won't you?"

"Yes." Then he thought of something. "Why do you want to know about women named Grace?"

"Just checking for coincidences."

"Coincidences?"

Prestwyck didn't answer, just stood to leave. John Smyth felt as if he had just run twenty miles. *Is this what you get for trying to be a good citizen?* he wondered. *That man actually made me feel guilty.*

Prestwyck was already on his way out the door. "Phone in the addresses tomorrow, eh?"

As Prestwyck walked back to his car, he felt satisfied. He felt he had made some progress, had managed to rattle Smyth at least. *Let Devorkian find fault with that interview,* he thought.

He felt less satisfied when he got back to the police station and was met at the door of his office by Harry Osnachuck. He gave Harry the list of Graces that Smyth had given him.

"I doubt if there is anything there, but check to make sure all of these women are still in the land of the living."

"Okay. Who are they?"

"All the Graces that John Smyth says he knows."

Osnachuck raised his thick eyebrows. "Anything else?"

"Not for now. How about the autopsy report? Is that in yet?"

"Lazinski just brought it in. There's a copy on your desk."

Prestwyck picked up a brown manila folder. "What's it say?"

Osnachuck shrugged. "Not much new. She was killed by a single shot to the head, died almost instantly. They recovered the bullet from inside the skull, by the way—a forty-four revolver. It evidently hit a bone and ricocheted—one reason we got so much damage near the entry wound. We'll try to match it by computer, but it will take a while."

"That's a long shot."

"No. She was shot at close range."

"I meant . . . never mind. Anything else?"

"She was killed about two or three weeks ago, was in good health, was not a drug user, was not a virgin, but was not pregnant. That's about it."

"Any other developments? Have we got any leads on identifying the woman?"

"No. The family of just about every missing woman in Canada has contacted us—okay, an exaggeration . . . but nothing fits."

"Could it be any of them?"

"It *could* be. We're checking, but nothing looks likely.

Take this one—a blonde woman, five foot eight, missing for three years. The family says maybe she dyed her hair."

"And shrank four inches? She didn't dye her hair, did she?"

"No."

"How about fingerprints?"

"We got some passable prints, ran them through the computer, but no matches. And no traceable fibers or anything under her nails. She had eaten about five hours before she died—a beef and lettuce sandwich, and fries. No trace of alcohol or drugs."

"And the drawing?"

"It looks like a drawing. Pretty general, and the artist says he could be wrong about the mouth—not much to go on, you know. We've circulated it on the police networks. No response yet. Should we give it to the papers and TV?"

"Not yet. The problem is if the mouth is wrong, somebody who knows the right woman might decide it's not her. Put it out if we don't hear something by next week. Today's Thursday. If we put it out now, it wouldn't hit the papers till Friday anyway, and everybody goes away weekends in the summer. We'd get more exposure on Monday or Tuesday."

"Okay."

"Heard anything from Devorkian and the city police?"

"No. Have you?"

"Not a thing. Must mean he can't match the dead woman up with anyone in his files. Maybe it means she's not from here and was just passing through on the Trans-Canada."

"Or was grabbed someplace else and dumped here."

"Yeah. Well, anyway, Devorkian must be as frustrated as—"

"As you are," Lazinski interrupted.

Prestwyck rested his forehead against his big hands. "Yeah," he muttered. "She has to be somebody!"

Apartment 307 in the Livingstone Apartments still lay silent and empty. The dust and the mail accumulated while the world rushed and roared by outside on the street and failed to notice.

The silence was suddenly shattered by a loud knocking on the door, a knocking which nevertheless failed to disturb the accumulating dust. Gladys Plumtre knocked again, paused, and knocked a third time. There was no answer. Shrugging her shoulders, she plodded away down the hall, dragging her overstuffed body back to the overstuffed furniture in her overstuffed apartment.

John Smyth was late for the "First and Third Thursday Winnipeg Grace Pastors and Wives Prayer Fellowship." The pastors of the Grace churches in Winnipeg and sometimes their wives got together every other Thursday to talk and pray. John Smyth usually attended—not only for the prayer, but also to catch up on what was happening in the churches.

This week, Ruby had decided to stay home with the kids—the youngest, Anne, had a cold—and John had stopped by a hardware store to pick up some materials for repainting the hallway. By the time the teenaged clerk managed to get his order right, he had entirely missed the opening talk—usually a meditation by one of the pastors on a short Bible passage. When he walked into the meeting, Jake Pendanz was already at the chalkboard writing down requests for prayer. Clint Granowski was talking.

"I want to ask for prayer for a number of people," he said. "First, there's my neighbor, Randy. I've been having real trouble getting to know him. He seems friendly on the surface, but he also seems to be avoiding us. Then there are John and Liz Freeman—they're an older couple who have moved in down the street. Carol and I have been to visit them a few times. They have just moved here from England. They have a daughter, Lucy, who married a Canadian a few years ago, and ever since she has been asking her parents to immigrate—promised to sponsor them and everything. Well, just after they got here, Lucy broke up with her husband and has taken off—they don't know where, but she seems to have left the city. Embarrassment, perhaps, because, you see, the parents aren't Christians, never went to church or anything, but Lucy and her husband had started going to Southside Charismatic Fellowship and were all enthused about it. They tried to get her parents to go, but now they've broken up. I guess she didn't know how to tell her mother and . . . Well, anyway, the Freemans, the parents, have been asking Carol and me all kinds of questions about different kinds of churches and whether prayers always get answered and so on. Pray for us that we'll know how to answer them."

Listening to Clint Granowski's requests, Smyth had to smile. The man and his wife sounded just alike.

"Okay," Jake Pendanz was saying. "That's John and Liz Freeman and their daughter, Lucy. Any other prayer requests?"

"Wait," Clint said. "I have one more. It's for Gary and Grace Drummond. I've mentioned them before. They have marriage problems, and they haven't been able to have kids. It's been kind of tough. Anyway, I was over to see him last night, and it seems Grace has left him again. I tried to get him to talk about it, but he seems really closed, unwilling to open up. If I could just get him to talk about their problems, maybe we could help them."

"Church planters always have lots of prayer requests," someone muttered.

"All right," Jake Pendanz said. "Anyone else?"

"I don't know whether you all read the paper this week,"

Harry Collins began. Harry was always bringing up news events and stories from outside the church and asking for prayer about them. Because he worked with people in the inner city, he sometimes served as a social conscience for the other pastors. "Anyway, there was a story in yesterday's paper about this woman they found murdered in the woods east of Winnipeg. There is far too much of that going on. There is too much violence against women. Here she is, somebody's daughter and maybe someone's sister or wife or even someone's mother, and now she's dead."

"Was she one of the people you work with, Harry?" someone asked.

"I don't know. She could be, I suppose. You see . . ."

Smyth hesitated a moment, weighing the options. His final decision was not so much a decision as a kind of offhand "Why not?" In a low voice, he murmured, "I may have seen it."

Harry stopped dead in midsentence. There was a long moment of silence. "You what?" he asked.

"I may have seen it. The murder."

This announcement was greeted by a hubbub of questions. How? When? Where?

"Well, it might not have been her. I mean, when I was flying back from Calgary, I saw—at least, I think I saw . . ."

Smyth haltingly told his story again. It was not any clearer this time than it had been when he had first told it to Sergeant Prestwyck. *And I'm supposed to be a master at writing orderly prose,* he sighed to himself when he had finished and the talk had gradually moved on to other prayer requests. He knew the other pastors would not forget. They would remember to pray about the situation, of course. But he knew that also for a long time he would be thought of as the editor who had seen a murder—maybe.

Chapter 9

FRIDAY, JULY 5

A key turned in the lock, and the door of Apartment 307 slowly and silently swung open. Annette Duclair stepped softly into the room. The early morning sun slanting in through the huge windows shone on her long, shining black hair. She stooped and picked up the pile of letters that the opening of the door had scattered across the floor, then placed them in a neat pile on the sideboard next to the single letter that was already there. Annette glanced carelessly at the address on that single letter: "Gladys Plumtre, Livingstone Apartments."

Uninterested, Annette walked to the hall closet, pulled out the vacuum cleaner, and began an energetic circuit around the apartment. The vacuuming done, she returned to the closet and selected three or four large white cloths from a bag hanging on the wall. She sprayed them with dust cleaner and proceeded to the living room, where she methodically began wiping all the flat surfaces free of their accumulated layers of dust. She picked up each knickknack and bookend, wiping them carefully. When she was finished in the living room, she continued her work with the same careful attention to detail in the hall and the bedroom.

Three hours later, Annette was finished. She had done an exceptionally good job, as had been requested. The carpet was immaculately groomed, and accumulated dust had been removed from every smooth surface in the apartment. She packed the vacuum cleaner away in the closet and dropped the dirty cloths into a hamper in the bedroom. Pausing by the front door, she picked up the phone and made a call. "It's Annette," she said. "I'm finished." She listened for a moment, said, "Okay," then slipped out the door. The door closed with a click behind her, leaving the apartment still and silent once more.

David Mackenzie had been walking around in indecision for two days. He had not been back to Grace Mission. He had found a discarded newspaper on Thursday, but there was little new about the woman who had been found murdered. Could it be Grace? If it was, what did it matter now? She was dead. But maybe he should help the police find whoever the scum was that killed her. Maybe if they knew who she was, it would help. But no, if they knew who she was, would they care, would they do anything about it? They didn't seem to have tried too hard so far. If they knew she was just a hooker, maybe they wouldn't try at all. But she wasn't just a hooker, David insisted. She was a woman, a beautiful, lovely woman, a woman he had . . . He shook his head. It didn't matter about him. What mattered was Grace. But what if it wasn't Grace? And if it wasn't, then where was she? Maybe someone would help him find her. If only he *knew* . . .

The questions went around and around in his head as David Mackenzie's steps wound around and around the downtown core. The more he walked and thought, the more tired and confused he became.

Friday evening, Clint Granowski went to see Gary Drummond again. This time he took Carol along, thinking maybe the presence of a woman might help Gary open up. He was wrong.

Drummond answered the doorbell and stood firmly in the doorway, looking down at the Granowskis.

"Hi, Gary," Clint began. "We just thought we would drop over. Do you mind if we come in?"

"Well, I don't know," Gary replied. "You were just here Wednesday. Nothin's changed."

Gary was not drunk, but he smelled like he had been drinking a bit. "I don't know why you keep coming," he said. "I ain't got much to say. Grace is gone, and she ain't coming back. I guess there ain't much point in it anymore."

"But, Gary," Clint said. "Maybe we could help. Maybe she would come back if we talked to her."

"She ain't coming back! I told you!" Gary shouted. "I don't know why you keep bugging me. Go away and leave me alone!" With surprising quickness, he turned and slammed the door. Clint and Carol were left standing on the doorstep, the fading echo of the slammed door wavering in their ears.

"Maybe it wasn't a good idea for me to come," she said at last.

"I don't know. For all we know, he might have reacted the same way regardless."

"It does look like he's made a decision of sorts."

"Yes, but let's keep praying. Nothing is hopeless."

"I only wish we knew where Grace has gone. If we could only talk to *her,* maybe she would be more receptive than he is."

Chapter 10

TUESDAY, JULY 9

Detective Devorkian sat in Sergeant Prestwyck's office, staring across the desk at Prestwyck.

"I asked you here," Prestwyck was saying, "so you can't say we're not cooperating fully."

"Have I ever said you weren't cooperating? Why are you so defensive?"

"I'm not defensive!"

What was there about Prestwyck that made him such an irresistible target, Devorkian wondered. Something awkward and vulnerable about him, despite his big frame? At any rate, Devorkian couldn't help himself. He liked to needle the other man, liked to rile him up. "Well, you know," he said, "I have another little theory. I think you've finally figured out that you're unable to solve this murder and so you want to pass it on to the Winnipeg police."

"That's the only theory you've come up with so far!"

Devorkian raised a sardonic eyebrow. "Don't get snippy

with me, Prestwyck. You've had the body for a week, and you haven't even been able to figure out whose it is, let alone who killed her."

"You've known about her for a week too, and I haven't seen you come up with anything. I take it you haven't been able to match her with any missing persons in Winnipeg?"

"Do you have any idea how many young women go missing in Winnipeg every week?"

"No, but I'll bet the number would be a lot lower if the Winnipeg police were able to find any of them."

He'd done it again. Devorkian backed off. "Okay, okay. This is getting us nowhere. Why did you really invite me down here?"

"You're right. We should get on with this. I've got a press conference scheduled in fifteen minutes."

"Press conference, eh? Going to give out more information? You may recall I said you'd have to do that from the beginning."

"Yeah, you told me." Prestwyck said. "The Winnipeg police are always right."

This time Devorkian ignored the sarcasm. "What are you going to tell the press?"

"Pretty well everything. We'll release the sketch, of course, and we'll give as full a description as we can, estimate the time of disappearance."

"Still estimated at two weeks before she was found?"

"Yeah. Everything we've looked at has just confirmed that."

"What else are you telling?"

"Well, we'll mention the white cloth and report on the necklace."

"Grace, eh?"

"Well, the one thing we plan to hold back is that we won't

release photos of the necklace, just mention that from jewelry she was wearing we think her name may be Grace."

"But it's a distinctive piece, right? Maybe someone will recognize it."

"You mean he will know that a Grace is missing but he won't report it unless he sees the exact necklace? Come on. We've got to save something to check out the story if anyone does come up with an ID."

"The RCMP have never heard of fingerprints or dental work?"

"I don't mean to identify the body. I'm thinking the killer might slip up and describe the necklace, assuming it's been shown to the public."

Devorkian grinned. "I suppose when the RCMP are on the job, your only hope is that you're dealing with a stupid criminal."

"Most of them are." For once Prestwyck didn't overreact. In fact, he seemed to be bending over backward to get along with Devorkian. *Must be getting frustrated with the case,* thought Devorkian.

The detective tried another tack. "You said 'he'. You're still assuming the murderer was a man."

"No. I just never learned to use politically correct language. I use 'he' to include all genders."

"Well, if you're looking for a 'he', I still think you may have had him originally."

"Who? Oh, Smyth? No, I checked him out. He seems legit. I've even been to his office. The magazine is real. Here's a copy."

Devorkian glanced briefly at the bright black-and-white cover and tossed it aside. "And does he know anyone named Grace?"

"I've checked that too. We've checked over the Graces he knows, and they all seem to be breathing still."

"The Graces he knows? What did you do? Ask him for a list?"

"Yup. I asked for a list and checked it out." Seeing Devorkian's smirk, he added quickly, "That's not *all* we'll check."

"And if he really did kill this Grace, do you really think he would tell you about her?"

"Probably not, but if we find out who Grace is and can prove he knew her, then we can ask him why he left her off his list."

"Not bad." Devorkian gave a grudging nod. "But it wouldn't stand up in court. Too close to entrapment. Pretty thin evidence."

"Maybe, but right now we'll take any evidence we can get."

"What are you talking about, evidence? You've got a body."

"And the bullet."

"Really?"

"Yeah, still embedded in the brain after ricocheting around inside her skull—a forty-four millimeter handgun."

"That's something. Will you release that information too?"

"No. That won't help identify her. It's another thing we're saving to help identify the murderer. He may not know we've got the bullet, and we don't want him to ditch the gun before we can try matching the ballistics. We are not even going to say how she died. Speaking of which, it's time for the press conference."

"You still haven't explained why you asked me here."

"I'm coming to that. This is an RCMP case, right?"

"That's what you keep saying."

"And I mean it. On the other hand, I want to solve this one. I'm not saying she was from Winnipeg. In fact, if you haven't identified her yet, the chances are pretty poor. Still, there is that chance."

"And?"

"And we know that sometimes people feel more comfortable coming to one police force than another."

"You mean the Canadian people don't trust you Mounties."

"More often your local flatfeet, but it works both ways. All I'm saying is I want to try every angle I can. What I'm proposing is that we make clear this is an RCMP case but also point out that we are cooperating with the city police, and if someone has information, they can contact either the RCMP or Detective Devorkian of the city police. Is that okay with you?"

Devorkian opened his mount for a smart remark, then thought better of it. He wanted the case solved too—even more than he liked needling Prestwyck. "Well, I haven't cleared it with the chief."

"You can phone him now if you want. We can delay the press conference a few minutes."

"No, that should be all right. The chief will probably give me a medal for bringing the RCMP around to cooperate with us for a change."

For once Prestwyck didn't rise to the bait. "You can sit at the end of the table in the press room. The chief may even give you a promotion for that."

This second press conference attracted more attention than the first one. Fifteen or twenty people had crammed into the press room. Prestwyck recognized many of them, but a half-dozen or so were strangers to him. He shot a glance at Devorkian to see if he recognized any of them, but Devorkian was staring at the assembled reporters with an expression that was at the same time intense, quizzical, and ultimately inscrutable. He did not return Prestwyck's look.

Prestwyck began. "I am Sergeant Prestwyck of RCMP

Division D here in Winnipeg. We are holding this press conference to update you on the case of the woman whose body was found on July 1, fifty kilometers east of Winnipeg. Despite extensive investigation, we have not been able to identify the woman. We have not been able to match her with any known missing person, either from southern Manitoba or other locations, although we are continuing to check numerous leads. Therefore, we are asking for the assistance of the public in identifying this woman. It is estimated that she died about the middle of June. There was some decomposition of the body. Corporal Gillespie is passing out a police artist's sketch of the woman's face. The police would appreciate it if you could give this drawing wide circulation. However, I would like to emphasize that due to the state of the body, some details of this drawing may be somewhat inaccurate. She is a Caucasian woman with short black hair, about one hundred sixty centimeters tall—that's five-foot-four-inches—weight about sixty-one kilograms—that's one hundred thirty-five pounds. As was stated one week ago, the police suspect foul play in this woman's death. She had no identification on her; however, from jewelry found on the body, we believe her name may have been Grace.

"The RCMP and the Winnipeg police are cooperating in this investigation. In fact, Detective Devorkian from the Winnipeg Police Department is here with us this morning. If anyone has information that might help us in identifying this woman, we would ask that they contact either the RCMP or the Winnipeg Police Department. That is the end of my statement. I will answer questions if you have any."

The questions were quick in coming, with Scott Ledyear leading the way:

"The Winnipeg police are involved. Does that mean you think the woman is from Winnipeg?"

"Not necessarily. Winnipeg is a big population base near where the woman was found, so we can't discount the possibility. On the other hand, she was found near the Trans-Canada Highway, so she really could be from anywhere. Even then, she may have passed through Winnipeg, so someone in the city may recognize her."

"Was she killed in the spot where she was found?"

"We are not releasing that information."

"Is Duane Goerzen a suspect in her death?"

"No. We believe he just found the body. We have no reason to connect him to the dead woman."

"How did the woman die?"

"We would rather not release that information until the family of the victim is found."

"Does that mean she was tortured or mutilated?"

"The evidence would not suggest that at this point."

"Was she sexually assaulted?"

"We will not be commenting on that."

"Then she *was* sexually assaulted?"

"No . . ."

The last questions had come from a woman Prestwyck did not recognize—a tall, chestnut-haired woman in a crisp designer suit. He was going to elaborate further on his answer, but he hesitated. "Are you a reporter?" he asked. "Do you have press credentials?" He turned for a second to glare at Corporal Gillespie.

"Do you mean only men are allowed to ask questions?" the woman replied.

"No, it is just that participation in press conferences is normally restricted to official representatives of the media."

"Is that so you can control the media?"

"No . . ."

"Yes, why don't you let her ask questions," Scott Ledyear

interrupted, obviously seeing another juicy sidebar to his main story developing.

"It seems to me she *is* asking questions," Prestwyck replied, making a recovery.

"But you're not answering them," Ledyear pressed.

"Okay, we do not suspect—"

The woman did not wait to hear his answer. "Why did it take you three weeks to start trying to find out this woman's identity?" she demanded.

"It didn't take us three weeks. The body was found only a week ago."

"But if the dead person was a man, you would have acted a lot quicker, wouldn't you? Since it's only a woman, you didn't really care too much, did you?"

"That's not true. We are doing a full investigation."

"Then why didn't you do anything for a whole week?"

"We have been doing something. It's just that we never suspected it would be so difficult to discover her identity. We're doing all we can. That's why I am personally heading up the investigation, why we asked Detective Devorkian—"

"How many women are involved in the investigation?"

"Well, I can't answer for the Winnipeg Police, but the RCMP has had women on the force for more than twenty-five years. Quite a few hold investigative positions. It just happens that at the moment we have no women in our division with the experience to handle a major murder investigation."

"But women have lots of experience in *being* murdered! Maybe if a woman was heading the investigation, something would have been done by now!"

Prestwyck toyed with retorting that the RCMP was not recruiting women with experience in being murdered because murdered women could not pass the physical exam. However, he was wise enough to know that would only make matters worse.

Half an hour later, Devorkian again sat in Prestwyck's office. Prestwyck had nabbed him at the end of the press conference, just as Devorkian was slipping out the side door, and insisted that he come back to his office. Yet for five minutes they had just sat there, with Prestwyck not saying a word.

Prestwyck was thinking, and he had come to a decision. He would never take a press conference again. That was what they paid Gillespie for.

At last he spoke. "That was close. For a while there, I thought I was not going to survive the press conference."

Devorkian said nothing.

"You know that woman, don't you?" Prestwyck continued.

Devorkian sighed. "Yes. She's Mary Alice Bruckner, founder and president of Women Against Risk."

"Why didn't you warn me?"

"Sorry. I didn't see her till the last minute, and by then it was too late."

"What's Women Against Risk?"

"A local group. Sort of a feminist enclave—although they've got their own special ax to grind. You catch the acronym? *W-A-R?* It describes them pretty well. They're on a crusade. They want to end all chance of women being victims of violence."

"And how do they propose to do that?"

"I don't know—by getting rid of all the men, I suppose."

"Would that work?"

"Only if the women who were left stayed away from each other."

"Better not say that in front of Mary Alice Bruckner."

"Well, they have a good point as far as it goes. They want

to end man's inhumanity to woman. It's just that the police have a broader goal."

"Which is?"

"We want to end man's inhumanity to man, man's inhumanity to woman, woman's inhumanity to man, and woman's inhumanity to woman."

"And you say *they* have an unrealistic goal."

Devorkian shrugged.

"The worst of it is I hate to see what this is going to do to my investigation. After that circus out there, do you think anybody is going to pay any attention to the description of the woman and help us identify her? We gave out all that information for nothing. And now we're going to be wasting a lot of time trying to defend ourselves in the media."

Chapter 11

WEDNESDAY, JULY 10

Sergeant Prestwyck's prediction was too pessimistic. The Wednesday morning edition of the *Winnipeg New Times,* for instance, featured the artist's sketch in the top center of the front page. The headline read, "Who's Grace?" Scott Ledyear's lead news story, although it vaguely suggested incompetence on the part of "the police," did include a complete description of the clues to the unknown victim's identity.

There was, however, an additional sidebar article entitled "If Women Ran the Police Force." It outlined in detail the criticisms that Mary Alice Bruckner had raised at the press conference and implied that she had outargued and outwitted the hapless police department. Evidently, Scott Ledyear had interviewed Mary Alice Bruckner after the press conference, for the article also reported some criticisms she hadn't raised there—including the charge that the police had a long history of ignoring crimes against women.

That last charge Prestwyck knew, of course, was especially preposterous, and police statistics would back him up. Still, all in all, he wasn't that unhappy with the coverage. Even that irrational sidebar could potentially help his investigation by drawing attention to the case. Maybe all he needed to do now was to sit back and wait for the information to come in.

The press coverage had been a success in another way too. Inviting Detective Devorkian to sit at the table during the press conference had been a great idea. Now, when criticism of the police handling of this case came in, much of it, especially that part originating in Winnipeg, would be directed toward the Winnipeg Police Department.

Prestwyck sighed, his satisfaction over the press coverage already draining away. This was shaping up to be a case where spreading the blame was just as important as grabbing the glory. Prestwyck wasn't sure they would ever discover who "Grace" was.

John Smyth had left for work a half-hour before and the kids were still sleeping, worn out from a late movie the previous night. At least Ruby hoped they were sleeping, because the house was uncharacteristically quiet. Determined to enjoy the peace instead of investigating, she brought the newspaper in from the front step, poured herself another cup of coffee, sat down at the breakfast table, and opened the newspaper. Grace's drawing leapt out at her. She began reading intently.

The doorbell chimed in the silence, startling her. At the door were two men she did not recognize, policemen in RCMP uniforms.

"Mrs. Smyth?"

"Yes?"

"I am Sergeant Prestwyck, and this is Corporal Osnachuck. Could we talk to you for a few minutes?"

Seated in the living room, Ruby wondered whether the policemen noticed how worn the carpet was. She also wondered what the children would think if they were to come downstairs and find two policemen there.

"Mrs. Smyth, have you seen this woman before?" Prestwyck handed her a copy of the same drawing that was in the newspaper. The copy in her hand was somewhat clearer. "Well?"

Ruby stared at the photo. "It's kind of general," she said. "It *could* be someone I know, but I really don't recognize her. I don't recall anyone who looks like this."

"Are you sure?"

"Yes, I'm sure I don't recognize it. It's the same picture that was in the paper, isn't it? This has to do with what my husband saw from the plane?"

Prestwyck allowed some time to pass before replying. "It may have," he said. "We're just checking." He paused again. "What *did* your husband see from the plane?"

"He thought he saw a woman being murdered, shot."

"Do you believe him?"

"Yes."

"How do you know he was in the plane?"

"Because he came home. How else could he get here? The night before, he phoned me from Calgary."

"How do you know he was in Calgary when he phoned?"

"He was at a convention. Lots of people would have seen him there. My husband does not lie to me."

Prestwyck changed tactics. "How many women do you or your husband know named Grace?" he asked.

"I don't know," she replied. "Half a dozen. Why? Didn't you ask John that? Didn't you get his answer?"

"Yes, but we just wondered if you could think of any others. Would you mind writing down a list of them?"

This is silly, Ruby thought. John had told her who he put on his list. Besides, was it legal for the police to ask for all this private information about her friends? Still, she thought it better to do as she was asked. "Okay," she said.

"All right. Write the names down for Corporal Osnachuck. And here is my card—in case you decide you have anything you want to tell me."

"Like what?"

"Oh, anything. If you remember another Grace, or if you remember who the woman in the drawing is. You can keep the copy."

Prestwyck left the house, got into the cruiser, and drove a few blocks toward the Grace Church denominational headquarters.

The good-looking blonde secretary was talking on the phone. Prestwyck stepped briskly past her and into Smyth's office. He jumped, as Ruby had done earlier.

"Good morning, Mr. Smyth. I have a couple more questions I would like to ask you. But first, do you mind if I use your phone to make a quick call?"

Prestwyck pulled the phone toward him and dialed. "Hello," he said. "This is Sergeant Prestwyck. Could I speak to Corporal Osnachuck for a moment, please?" There was a short pause. "Osnachuck? I'm here. Okay."

Prestwyck put down the phone, turned to Smyth, and smiled.

Harry Osnachuck put down the phone at his end. "Thank you, Mrs. Smyth," he said. "Are you sure you can't think of any more Graces?"

Ruby nodded her head. "I'm sure."

"Seven Graces," Osnachuck murmured as he read through the list. "Are any of them the woman in the picture?"

"No."

"Could any of them be the woman in the picture?"

"Uh . . . no."

"Which of these women has your husband had an affair with?"

Ruby's jaw dropped. "N-n-none of them," she stammered.

"Are you sure?"

"Yes!"

"How many affairs has he had in the past?"

"Never! I mean . . . none." Her face flushed as anger flared. "Exactly what are you trying to do here?"

Osnachuck smiled, ignoring her show of temper. "Thank you for your help," he said. "If there is something you haven't told us, you will let us know, won't you?" He turned to go, then paused in the doorway. "Oh, one more thing. Don't phone your husband right away. He'll be busy talking to us for the next half-hour or so."

The shutting of the door echoed through the house. Still fuming, Ruby watched as Osnachuck walked down their walk to the street, then turned in the direction of her husband's office.

"Did you see the newspaper this morning?" Prestwyck asked.

"Uh . . . no."

"Who is this woman?" Prestwyck passed a copy of the police drawing over to Smyth.

Smyth looked at the photo. "I don't recognize her," he said at last. "It looks vaguely familiar, but it's kind of general. It could be a lot of people."

"Which one of the Graces on your list is she?"

"Uh . . . none of them."

"So you did leave someone off the list? What's her last name?"

"I—I didn't leave anyone off. I—I don't know her. Is this the dead woman?"

Prestwyck was watching Smyth intently. "Can you prove you were in Calgary the night of June fifteenth?"

"Yes. I was at the conference until ten that evening. I've got the hotel receipt and the plane ticket stub. They would be in our financial files. Do you want to see them?"

"Later."

Prestwyck met Osnachuck on the street. "Did you learn anything?" he asked.

"She says she's never seen the woman, and she swears her husband is faithful to her."

"Do you believe her?"

"So far. I've no reason to think otherwise. But she seems rattled."

"Yeah, she would be, either way."

"What about the husband?"

"Smyth says he has documented evidence he was in Calgary from June fourteenth to June sixteenth."

"Will it stand up? Did you see it?"

"No, but I'm not sure it matters. We have only an approximate date of death. He could have killed her and stashed the body on Friday or Monday, or killed her on Friday and hid the body somewhere until Monday. It was moved, remember."

"So we haven't gotten anywhere, really. Maybe we'll get some responses from the press coverage."

"Oh, I wouldn't say we haven't made *any* progress. The husband seems rattled too. Maybe somebody will make a mistake."

It was later that evening, after he came home from work, that Gary Drummond finally saw Scott Ledyear's second article. He sat in his silent living room, reading it over and over, not even noticing that his hands had started to tremble.

At the same time, in the Livingstone Apartments, Gladys Plumtre was reading the same article. She read it over twice, slowly, without stopping.

"It could be," she said to herself. "It could."

Her left hand reached out for the phone.

Chapter 12

THURSDAY, JULY 11

Hello."

"Hello. Louise?"

"Yes."

"It's Mary Alice."

"Oh, yes."

"Did you see the newspaper yesterday?"

"Yes . . . you mean about that poor girl who was murdered?"

"Yes, of course. It's another case of a woman being killed and the police not doing anything about it."

There was a slight murmur from the other end of the line.

"Well, we're going to do something about it," Mary Alice continued. "This Saturday, we're having a big rally at the Legislature. Ten-thirty."

"Well, okay."

"What's wrong? You don't seem sure about this. Don't you believe in what we're doing? If we don't act, nothing is going to be done again!" Her voice softened into a persuasive purr. "We have to put a stop to this terror against women, Louise. It's our lives and our daughters' lives and our sisters' lives on the line. We could be next."

Louise was silent for a long minute, then spoke in a faint voice. "Yes, I . . . I know. It's not that. It's . . . well, I've been sitting here reading the paper and looking at that picture. And—"

"Sitting and crying isn't going to change anything. That's what we have been doing for centuries, and the beating and the killing and raping go—what do you mean? Do you mean you recognize the woman? Do you know who Grace is?"

"Well, I don't know. . . . I mean, that is what I have been trying to decide. I don't know if it's her or not. You see, I have this neighbor across the road. The picture . . . I don't know. I mean, it *could* be her. Her husband, Gary, he drinks, and well . . . I think once he hit her. And, well, I haven't seen her for a while, like a few weeks or something, and that might not mean it's her 'cause she left once before and . . . anyway, I don't want to say anything because what if it isn't her? I mean, she could still be there and just be sick or something and . . ."

"What's her name?" Now Mary Alice's tone was abrupt, stern.

"Well, that's just it . . . I mean, her name *is* Grace. The picture—I don't know, it could be. But the name . . . it's Grace, Grace Drummond."

"Grace! Louise Crocker! You know this and haven't done anything about it!? Sometimes I can't believe you're my cousin, and Sarah Jane's cousin! We've got to act, to do something. Once again, the police sit on their fat butts and we have to do their work for them. Stay right there. I'll pick you up in fifteen minutes."

"But . . ."

But Mary Alice had hung up.

Louise Crocker was a petite, middle-aged housewife, just over five feet tall, with mousy brown hair and dark-rimmed glasses. She stood in her living room watching through the picture window as Mary Alice's blue Honda pulled into the driveway, but she didn't wait for her cousin to come to the door. Moving slowly but deliberately, she locked her door and walked out to get into the car.

She didn't speak until they were pulling out of the driveway. "Mary Alice . . . ?"

"Yes."

"I . . . um . . . I'm not too sure about this. I mean, what if it isn't her and they arrest him and he's not guilty?"

"Well, if it isn't her, then we'll find out. But what if it is? We have to do this. And besides, he beats her anyway, right?"

"I—I think so."

"Then he deserves to be arrested, right? If he's arrested now, maybe we will *prevent* a murder instead of just catching someone afterward."

"I suppose so," Louise mumbled.

"Louise, you have to tell what you know. We're at war here, remember. This man has killed a woman, and you're worrying about inconveniencing him?"

The blue Honda pulled into a parking spot near the Winnipeg Police station just off Main Street. The two women got out and walked down the street, pushing past some police officers on their way into the building. Mary Alice marched purposefully; Louise walked wordlessly at her side. They stopped in front of the front desk.

"We have some information on the man who murdered Grace," Mary Alice announced.

"Mary Alice . . ." Louise whispered.

Mary Alice ignored her and went right on talking to the female officer at the desk. "We want to talk to the detective in charge of the case."

"Mary Alice . . ." Louise whispered again.

"We want to speak directly to the detective in charge, and we need your help to get us in to see him. We have important information that will solve the case."

"Mary Alice . . ."

"Detective Devorkian is busy interviewing someone else," the policewoman said.

"Mary Alice," Louise whispered again. "That man over there—that's Gary Drummond!"

The policewoman turned around and looked over to a glassed-in office where a tall, distinguished-looking man in a neat, dark suit was talking with an equally tall but younger man in blue jeans.

"Well, you certainly took your time getting here. I phoned last night. Aren't you interested in finding out who that woman was? When I saw that picture in the paper, I recognized her right off. I turned to Fred and I said, 'Fred, that woman they found, I bet that that's Grace Hutchinson. It looks just like her. No wonder she didn't pay her rent this month. She's been murdered.' Murdered, that's what I said. And to think she lived right here in this building! Why, she could have been killed right here. It could have been anyone. It could have been me. He could have killed us all in our beds while we slept. Have you caught him yet—the killer, I mean? I bet he was one of those criminals out on a leave or parole or something. Why, he could be back in prison right now, laughing at you."

Sergeant Prestwyck shuddered slightly at the thought as the hefty apartment manager led him and Osnachuck down the corridor of the Livingstone Apartments. But despite her words, Gladys Plumtre seemed strangely cheerful, undaunted by the possibility of a murder in her building.

"Here we are," she announced, pointing her handful of keys at one of the doors. "Apartment 307."

"Wait, Mrs. Plumtre. Have you been in this apartment?"

"Sure, a few times. We didn't see her socially, but I've been there for rent and once when the toilet backed up . . ."

"No, Mrs. Plumtre. I mean have you been in the apartment in the last month? Did you come in here last night, after you decided she might be the missing woman?"

"No. I phoned the police right away. By the way, why did it take so long for you to get here?"

"We have had a lot of tips, Mrs. Plumtre."

"About Grace Hutchinson? Other people have phoned you about her?"

"No. Not that I know about. They were tips about other people, other women who might be the murdered woman, people who saw something suspicious."

"Well, why did you take so long to get *here?*"

"As I said, we have had a lot of leads to follow up, and I wasn't on duty last night. They left the most important leads for me to follow up. I'm the one in charge of this case."

"But you're only a sergeant. Don't the RCMP have any detectives? Maybe I should have phoned the city police. No wonder you haven't found out who the murderer is."

"Mrs. Plumtre, I assure you I am fully qualified to head up this investigation. 'Detective' is a rank in the city police; it's not a rank we have in the RCMP. Believe me, I have full authority." Prestwyck shook his head. This was not working. Gladys Plumtre didn't even seem to be impressed that he had called her an important lead. "Now tell me," he continued, "when was the last time you saw Grace Hutchinson?"

"Oh, I don't know. Maybe a month ago. I don't see some of the tenants for weeks sometimes, but it doesn't mean they're not here. I don't remember the last time I saw Grace, really. It was just that she didn't pay her rent this month. She's never done that before."

"The rent was due on the first?"

"The second, actually, because of the holiday. When she didn't pay, I just assumed she might have been away and would be back in a couple of days. I waited awhile, then I came up and knocked on her door a couple of times, but she wasn't here. I finally left her a note on Tuesday, but I still haven't heard from her."

"Were you worried?"

"Not a lot. Every month there's three or four tenants who don't pay the rent on time. They're just away or they forgot, usually. It takes a few days to track them down, but they usually pay. It's a good building—quiet, responsible tenants for the most part. We've never had a murder here before, not even a robbery."

"Okay, Mrs. Plumtre. Excuse me." Prestwyck reached past her and knocked on the door.

After several seconds, when no one answered, he knocked again, then again.

"Doesn't seem to be home. All right, Mrs. Plumtre, would you unlock the door for us, please?"

When she had done so, he slid his foot into the opening, grasped Mrs. Plumtre by the elbow, and said, "Thank you very much, Mrs. Plumtre. We'll take it from here."

The apartment manager, who had been on the point of going in, strangled a half-gasp. "Oh . . . all right." She turned and started back down the hall.

"Thank you, Mrs. Plumtre. You did the right thing," Prestwyck said to her retreating back. She did not seem to hear. "Now, let's check this out."

Prestwyck and Osnachuck slid through the half-open door, and Prestwyck eased the door closed with a gloved hand. Then he and Osnachuck looked around. Scattered on the floor near the door were several letters and a folded piece of paper.

"Mail. Been gone a while," Prestwyck muttered. "No, don't touch it. I don't want anything in this apartment touched yet. That"—he indicated the folded piece of paper on the floor—"is probably the note from Mrs. Plumtre. And look, there are more letters here on the table. Somebody's been here, possibly not Grace Hutchinson. Maybe someone's been apartment sitting."

"Look at that letter. It's addressed to Mrs. Plumtre."

"The missing rent money? Hmm. Doesn't mean too much. Could go either way. She might have gotten it ready, gone away, and forgotten to give it to her."

"Or she might have gotten it ready early and been murdered before she had a chance to give it to her."

"Yes. Someone has been here, I think. The dust isn't very thick for a place that's been empty a month."

They looked briefly through the kitchen, living room, and bedroom. Everything was neat and organized. Grace Hutchinson apparently kept things tidy.

"Do you see any pictures, Osnachuck?"

"Pictures? There are some on the walls."

"Yes, but they're scenery. I mean pictures of people—of Grace Hutchinson, of her family."

"Oh, I see what you mean. No, there don't seem to be any."

Prestwyck stepped over to the closet and pulled the door

open. "How many suitcases does a woman normally own, Osnachuck?"

"I don't know. A couple?"

"There're two suitcases and an overnight bag here. Would she have others? Could she have gone away?"

"I don't know. The apartment's in pretty good shape. Maybe she isn't missing at all. Maybe she's just at work or something."

"Yes, but that looks like more than one day's mail on the floor. And why hasn't she paid the rent? We definitely need to get the place dusted for prints."

"For the killer's or for Grace Hutchinson's?"

"For Grace Hutchinson's first, then maybe a killer's. We've got to find out who that dead woman is." Prestwyck sounded resentful, as if it were the body's fault that it refused to be identified. "Get Mrs. Plumtre back here."

"Are you going to ask her to identify the body?"

"No, I'm not ready for that. She didn't see the woman for months at a time, remember."

Osnachuck paused at the door. "Well, at least one thing," he said. "If this is the missing woman, then that religion writer guy couldn't have seen her get shot in here."

"Yes, but she wasn't shot here. No one was." Prestwyck gestured down at the pristine carpet. "There's no blood."

A few minutes later, Corporal Osnachuck ushered Mrs. Plumtre into Grace Hutchinson's apartment, taking care to push the door wide open so she wouldn't touch it.

"Thank you for coming back," Prestwyck said in his most conciliatory manner. "Please don't touch anything. You have given us a very important lead, and we are going to investigate thoroughly."

"You mean, you think it's her?"

"We aren't sure yet, Mrs. Plumtre. But there are a couple more questions I would like to ask you. First, see that letter on the table? Don't touch it. Is that Grace Hutchinson's handwriting?"

"I think so. I don't know. About all I've seen is her signature on the checks."

"How did she usually pay her rent?"

"Like I said, by check. She would bring it down personally the first of every month."

"No envelope?"

"Not usually, no. Most of our tenants are like that."

"Do you know how many suitcases Grace Hutchinson has?"

"No. Why should . . . ?"

"That's okay, Mrs. Plumtre. There's no reason you should know. Now, I don't suppose you would have any pictures of Grace Hutchinson, but do you know if she had any of herself?"

"I never really noticed. I wasn't here that often."

"Again, that's fine, Mrs. Plumtre."

"Well, maybe she threw them out. Her husband died a year ago, and she was pretty broken up about it. People do strange things sometimes. Say, you don't think she might have committed suicide?"

"It's not likely. Did she have any other family?"

"Not that I know of. She never said."

"Do you know any of her friends? Could she have mentioned a name? Was she friendly with any of the other tenants?"

"No, I don't think so. I don't know."

"Do you know who her dentist is?"

"Her dentist? No."

"Where does she work?"

"Oh, I don't think she has a job."

"She doesn't?"

"Well, she never said, and we never saw her go out regularly in the mornings."

"How does she get her money?"

"I don't know. She seems to have plenty. I think maybe her husband was rich."

"Why would you think that?"

"I don't know. Something she said once, but I don't really remember."

"Okay. Does Grace Hutchinson have a car?"

"Yes. Parks in the underground parking."

"What kind of car is it?"

"A little red one. I don't know the make."

"Do you know the license number?"

"It's down in my records. I can tell you what parking space she's in too. They're numbered."

"Good. Can you give that information to Corporal Osnachuck? And one more thing: We want to thoroughly investigate this apartment. That means neither you nor anyone else can come in here under any circumstances. Do you understand?"

"That means the cleaning lady too?"

"Cleaning lady? She has a cleaning lady?"

"Cleaning service, actually—Maids in a Row, they're called. They come in once a month or so, near the beginning of the month, I think. Give the place a thorough cleaning—though I can't think why she doesn't just do it herself."

"Cleaning lady!" Prestwyck muttered to himself when she was gone. Then added a few well-chosen swear words.

Prestwyck was waiting in the hall when Osnachuck came back. "A red Honda, license ADW 369, parking space number twenty-five," Osnachuck reported. "Want to check it out?"

Prestwyck nodded. They rode the elevator down to the

parking garage in silence. Prestwyck pulled open the heavy metal door to the garage and began walking down the lines of cars.

"There it is," Osnachuck said. "Number twenty-five."

They slowly circled the car without touching it, peering in the windows.

"Could be," Prestwyck said. "Dust's pretty thick on it. Hasn't been driven for a while." He straightened up.

"What are you going to do now?"

"Take that apartment apart. And the car."

"Should I phone the forensics team?"

"Yeah, but just tell them to get ready. We have to make a little trip first."

"Where?"

"We're supposed to be working in cooperation with the Winnipeg police on this one, remember? This apartment is in the city. So we need to drop in on Detective Devorkian."

"Do you think he'll want to take over the search of the apartment?"

"Nah. That's just extra work for his crew. He'll probably be content to let us have this one."

"Detective Devorkian, there's someone here I think you should talk to."

Devorkian looked at Constable Hansson irritably. He didn't like to be interrupted in the middle of an interrogation. Couldn't she see he was busy? For a fleeting moment, he wondered if the female officer was in league with those crazy women trying to take over his investigation. The serious look on her face convinced him otherwise. "Who is it?" he asked.

"Well . . ." Constable Hansson glanced hesitantly at the tall man in blue jeans who sat across the table from Devorkian.

"All right," Devorkian said. "I'm sorry to interrupt this, Mr. Drummond. I'll be right back."

Down the hall a few paces, the policewoman explained in a low voice. "There's a woman here who says she thinks she can identify the dead woman."

"Why didn't you just have someone take her statement and tell her we'll get back to her? You didn't need to interrupt me for that."

"Yes, but I think she thinks it's Gary Drummond's wife."

Devorkian whistled softly. "What do you mean you think? Why didn't you ask her?"

"She didn't really want to talk to me. At least, the woman with her didn't want her to talk to me. She insisted on talking only to the detective in charge." Hansson paused. "I think the woman with her is Mary Alice Bruckner."

"Oh," Devorkian said.

"I've put them in the interrogation room at the end of the hall."

"Okay, thanks, Hansson. I'll go talk to her. Have Sergeant Hosschuk stay with Drummond. And get Drummond a coffee. Explain I'll be only a few minutes. I don't want him getting spooked. And then come down to the interrogation room with me."

As Hansson walked away, Devorkian muttered to himself, "I'm not afraid to interrogate a murderer, but I'm not about to be alone in a room with Mary Alice Bruckner."

A couple of minutes later, he breezed into the interrogation room followed closely by Hansson. He flashed a broad but shallow smile at the two women sitting there—one small and timid-looking, the other tall, well-dressed, and familiar.

"Good morning. I'm Detective Devorkian. I believe you've met Constable Hansson. And you're Mary Alice Bruckner, aren't you?" He shook hands with her first. "I remember you were at the press conference on Tuesday."

Mary Alice looked at him coldly. "Yes. This is my cousin, Louise Crocker. She lives on Mapleleaf Street, and she has something important to tell you, but first we want to know that you are going to take what we are going to say to you seriously."

"Ms. Bruckner, if I wasn't going to take you seriously, I wouldn't have interrupted an interrogation to talk with you. I am going to take what Ms. Crocker has to say very seriously."

"What interrogation? Have you arrested Gary Drummond?"

Devorkian stopped in the act of settling into a chair. "No," he said carefully. "We have not arrested Gary Drummond. Do you have evidence to suggest that we should?"

He had been looking at Louise, but it was Mary Alice who responded: "Then why is he here?"

"He is here to answer some questions," Devorkian replied slowly. "We really have only begun our interrogation, so I'm not sure yet what he will have to say."

"Why did you bring him here?" Mary Alice demanded.

"I would rather not say at the moment. That is really police business."

"Police business is catching the men who torture and murder women, Detective! If you weren't so busy protecting police interests and worried more about protecting innocent women, maybe we women wouldn't have to do your work for you."

Devorkian took a slow, deliberate breath. "I appreciate any help you can give us, Ms. Bruckner, but it's not going to *be* help if you don't tell us what you know. I hope that what you have to say will help us to interrogate Gary Drummond properly."

He turned to Louise Crocker again. Louise hesitated.

"All right, Detective," Mary Alice decided, "but we're not just going to give you information and then go away and let you find some excuse to let that murderer off. We'll be watching what you do, and you'd better do something with this information. Go ahead, Louise. Tell him."

"Well," Louise began hesitantly. Then she took a deep breath and plunged in. "Gary's wife is named Grace, and the picture in the paper—well, it isn't a very good likeness, but it could be her. And I haven't seen her for a few weeks, and I think he drinks, and I think he beats her."

"How do you know the Drummonds?" Devorkian asked.

"I live right across the street from them."

"Do you know them well?"

"Not well. I've talked to Grace a few times."

"How long have you lived across the street?"

"About seven years, but the Drummonds have been there only two years."

"What do you mean he drinks? How much? How do you know?"

"What do you mean, how does she know?" Mary Alice Bruckner broke in. "It's obvious he's another drunken, violent husband. How often does he have to get drunk and beat his wife before you think it's a crime?"

"Ms. Bruckner, I'm a police officer. I can't lay charges unless I have some evidence—hard evidence. Ms. Crocker, did you ever see Mr. Drummond drunk?"

"Well, a couple of times I could hear him yelling—the windows were open. And at least once he came outside, and he seemed unsteady—he almost fell over."

"Was he drunk, or could he have tripped?"

"Of course he was drunk," Mary Alice snapped.

"Ms. Bruckner, have you ever seen Mr. Drummond before this morning?"

"No. But—"

"Then please let Ms. Crocker answer the questions. If she ever comes into court, she can't have you on the stand to answer her questions for her. Now, Ms. Crocker, are you sure Gary Drummond was drunk?"

"I think so. He staggered several times, not just once."

"Good." That was for Mary Alice's benefit. "Did Grace ever say that Gary got drunk?"

"Well, she told me once she didn't like him drinking because it made him angrier."

"Did she ever tell you he had hit her?"

"Not exactly. But she did say she was afraid of men when they got angry. She said men. And she didn't exactly say she was afraid of Gary, but she did say he got angry."

"What did he get angry about?"

"The usual things. Work. If dinner was late. But I think what really made him angry was that she wasn't getting pregnant."

"Typical male," Mary Alice snorted. "Only wants a woman to make meals and make babies."

Devorkian ignored her. "Why wasn't she getting pregnant? Weren't they having sex? Or was she using birth control?"

"No. I think she wanted a baby too. She said once I was lucky to have my two children. I think maybe she just couldn't."

"Why not?"

"Don't badger her, Detective," Mary Alice said. "Don't you know how babies are made?"

Devorkian was getting frustrated with the three-way conversation. He was having trouble remembering who was interrogating whom. "Do you know specifically why the Drummonds were having trouble making babies? Was it infertility or a low sperm count? What I want to know is whether it was his problem or hers. Could he have been angry at her because *she* couldn't get pregnant? Did she ever say?"

"She didn't tell me that. We weren't really that close."

"All right. When did you see her last?"

"I don't know exactly. It was about a month ago."

"Do you remember what Mrs. Drummond was doing the last time you saw her? Did she say anything?"

"I don't really remember. I used to see her quite often in passing—taking out the garbage, walking to the store, sweeping the step, that sort of thing. It's just that I know I haven't seen her for a while."

"Did she ever hint that she might leave Mr. Drummond?"

"She never said so, but once before she disappeared for a month or so. I think she left him then—or maybe she was just away."

"Thank you, Ms. Crocker. Is there anything else you can tell us?"

"Perhaps now you can tell us why you brought in Mr. Drummond?" Mary Alice demanded.

"Oh, we didn't bring him, Ms. Bruckner. He came in on his own, to report his wife missing." He held up his hand to stop the expected flow of words. "But believe me, now that Mr. Drummond is here, we are certainly going to ask him some questions. Some pointed questions."

"Now, Mr. Drummond," Devorkian said as he walked into the room. "I'm sorry for the interruption. It really was unavoidable. Thank you, Hosschuk."

Gary Drummond looked up, startled, as if he had been deep in thought and had not noticed Devorkian approaching. The stocky, blond Sergeant Hosschuk made a quick exit.

Sitting down opposite Drummond, Devorkian continued. "Mr. Drummond, you say you came here because you think the body we found might be your wife's. Now, what makes you think that?"

"I didn't say I *think* it's my wife. I said I'm afraid it *might* be my wife. You see, she left me some time ago."

"When, exactly?"

"Let's see. Do you have a calendar? It was the morning of June sixteenth, a Sunday."

Devorkian's face did not change, except for a light that began to glimmer in his eyes. "Did she have a reason to leave you?"

"Yeah, I guess so. We had a fight the night before."

"What about?"

"Nothing important. We . . . we just get on each other's nerves. Little stuff, you know. I don't even remember what started it that time."

"So you've quarreled before?"

"Yeah."

"And has your wife ever left you before?"

A long pause. "Yeah, once."

"Where did she go that time?"

"Back to her parents in Alberta."

"Do you think that's where she went this time?"

"No."

"Have you checked? Did you phone them?"

"No." For someone who had come in voluntarily, Gary Drummond was slow about volunteering information.

"Why didn't you call them?"

"I—I don't think . . . That's not where she said she was going."

"And where *did* she say she was going?"

"She said she was going to Johnny Cockerill."

"And who's Johnny Cockerill?"

"I don't know. An old boyfriend. I don't know exactly who

he is. She only started talking about him the past few weeks. She said . . . she said she was going to leave me and go back to him because he would treat her right."

"And would he?"

"Like I said, I don't know. I don't know who he is."

"Does he live in Winnipeg?"

"I don't know. I don't know anything about him."

"Where's your wife from?"

"Alberta. Drumheller."

"What are her parents' names?"

"John and Kathy Redcliffe."

"They still live in Drumheller?"

"Yes."

"What's their phone number?"

"I don't remember. We don't get along too well. I didn't bring it with me."

"Is Johnny Cockburn still living in Drumheller?"

"I don't know where he lives. I don't even know when she met him."

Devorkian noted that Drummond had not noticed the change from Cockerill to Cockburn. It might mean something, or it might not. "What other places has your wife lived?"

"Just Drumheller and here. She came and stayed with an aunt to look for a job—there's not too much in Drumheller. We met here."

"So she must have known Johnny either here or in Drumheller?"

"I guess. Probably Drumheller. I met her soon after she moved here."

"Could she have met him after you got married? Was she seeing someone else?"

Drummond shrugged his shoulders. "I don't know. I don't think so. Maybe."

"Do you want her back?"

"Ye-es." It was half a word, half a croak.

"Then why didn't you phone her parents?"

"She said she wasn't going there."

"You could have tried."

"We—we don't get along too well. I'm not sure they would talk to me."

Devorkian wasn't sure where to take the interrogation next. Constable Hansson saved him from making a decision by appearing in the doorway. "Sergeant Prestwyck of the RCMP is here to see you."

"Prestwyck? What does he want?"

Prestwyck, it turned out, wanted Devorkian's assent to an RCMP search of Grace Hutchinson's apartment. Devorkian was glad enough to give it. Grace Hutchinson didn't interest him much, anyway. He had a more likely lead in Gary Drummond, and he didn't want to tie up his forensic teams elsewhere.

"Sure," he said. "Go ahead. I'll send one of my men over with you. I will point out, however, that this is in Winnipeg, as I said from the beginning."

"So you do believe John Smyth saw something."

"I believe in Grace's body, which was found two weeks ago. But why fight over it? We've got lots of other crimes to solve anyway."

"Have *you* got any leads on the Grace case?"

Devorkian considered for a moment. Prestwyck had told him about Grace Hutchinson, and he needed Prestwyck's cooperation because Prestwyck had the body and other evidence. He decided to tell him the bare minimum.

"We have a man named Gary Drummond. I haven't finished talking to him yet—in fact, I should get back to him right now—so I don't really know if it'll amount to anything. He says his wife's named Grace, and she left him about a month ago, but he thinks she could be with some other man. He isn't sure she's the woman in the police drawing."

"Are you going to bring him to see the body?"

"I'd like to. It might at least eliminate the possibility."

"Or it might mean that we've solved the question of Grace's identity." Prestwyck was getting interested.

"Yes, but the body is not in good condition. What if Drummond says yes and it isn't her?"

"Or what if he says no and it is?"

"That would be tricky, because I would want to search his house for the gun."

"You think he did it?"

"Not necessarily. The husband's just the obvious suspect."

"Well, hold him on suspicion and get a search warrant."

"While you get one for Grace Hutchinson's place?"

"You have a point. The judge might get the idea that we're just fishing and turn us down for both warrants. So . . . we'll use different judges."

"That'll work for now, but there might be trouble when they find out."

"Naw, we'll just say the RCMP and city police didn't communicate very well."

"They'll believe that, but it might not satisfy them."

"Let's worry about that later."

"Are you going to show the body to the apartment manager?"

"No way. That lady would identify her if Grace Hutchinson was seventy-five years old, seven feet tall, and weighed three hundred pounds. That or have a heart attack and sue us. I'm not risking it for now."

"Yes, same reason I sent Mary Alice Bruckner home." That ought to discourage Prestwyck from getting too interested in Gary Drummond.

"Mary Alice Bruckner? She was here? Why didn't you warn me—or shoot her or something?"

"She was here with another woman—said it was her cousin. The woman lives across the street from the Drummonds."

"Why did she come here?"

"Same reason as Drummond, to report Grace Drummond missing."

"Are you going to show the body to the neighbor?"

"Not as long as Mary Alice Bruckner is around. She's already made up her mind and can't be bothered with the facts. Told me she'll be watching what we do."

"Scary thought."

News is hard to come by when you live on the street. That's why it was Thursday afternoon and David Mackenzie had still not heard any more about the body that had been found outside of town. He had been pondering what to do about Grace for three weeks now, and he had grown tired of it. That had been his trouble. He had never been able to stay with anything very long. It was just one more failure, one more loss for which he found no satisfactory explanation, one more question for which he never found an answer. It was like being back in school again.

Then it struck him—literally. He was wandering through a back alley looking for anything or nothing when a copy of Wednesday's *New Times* plastered itself against his legs—finally an answer blowing in the wind. He peeled the paper from his legs and folded it carefully. It would serve as a little more padding against the cold cement that night. As he made the last fold, Grace's picture struck out at his eyes. He unfolded the paper, read a few lines, and refolded it quickly. Glancing over his shoulder, he scurried away down the alley.

Two blocks away, a large, blue garbage bin was shoved into the end of a *U*-shaped indentation in a dirty brick building, beside a loading dock. The bin was rarely pushed back in all the way, and the space behind it made a good cubbyhole for a homeless person to sleep in or read in undisturbed. Crouched there, David read the story about Grace over slowly five times, examining the police drawing carefully. Grace. It was Grace.

David sat and pondered a long time. Then he handled the situation the same way he had handled every other difficult situation in his life. He folded the paper carefully and stuffed it into a crack behind a weathered piece of plywood covering a dirty window. He peeked out, and when he was sure no one was looking, he scrambled out and scurried down the alleyway, heading for the cheap bars of Main Street. He had only a few dollars, but he knew places and people where, when he really needed to, he could stretch those meager resources into two days of forgetfulness.

"Now, Mr. Drummond, I must warn you. The body I am going to show you had been lying in the woods for two weeks before it was found. It will be very difficult for you to look at it. I ask you not to concentrate on the face—it will likely be unrecognizable. If you feel . . . sick . . . you can use one of those bowls. Now, are you ready?"

They were standing in a cold stainless-steel room. The air reeked of formaldehyde and disinfectant and something else. Mortality perhaps.

Gary Drummond took a deep, deep breath and nodded.

A stainless-steel drawer was pulled out of the wall by a man in a white coat. In one swift movement, Devorkian whipped away a white sheet, revealing a white form underneath.

The gesture was melodramatic, but effective. Drummond gasped, teetered, but caught himself. His eyes were riveted on where the woman's face had been.

"Don't concentrate on the face, Mr. Drummond. Look at the whole body. Was this your wife, Mr. Drummond?"

Drummond's eyes remained riveted on the woman's missing face. "She—she's been shot," he stammered.

"Do you think so?"

"Yes. The face—it's . . . it's . . . it's missing." Gary Drummond waved his hand helplessly in the general direction of the dead woman.

"How do you know she wasn't stabbed or attacked with an ax, Mr. Drummond? What makes you think she was shot?"

"I—I don't know. The way the mess is sort of like a crater.. You didn't tell me. . . . Was it just a shot . . . ?"

"But you do recognize your wife, Mr. Drummond?"

Drummond forced his eyes from the face to slide over the rest of the body. Glazed, they then widened. He opened his mouth, but no words came out. He shook his head crazily from side to side. "No," he gasped. "It's not her."

"Not her? Why not, Mr. Drummond? Why isn't it her? Why isn't it like her?"

"I don't know . . . the shape . . . the hair.. . ."

"The hair is matted. But it is your wife, isn't it, Mr. Drummond?"

The head wagged crazily again, and the jaw worked. Drummond gulped, shivered, and then seemed to catch hold of himself. "No," he said. "The hair isn't quite the right color . . . or length. The arms are too thin. . . . The . . ." Drummond faltered and stared. A gray light appeared in his eyes. A light of recognition—Devorkian was sure of it.

Drummond turned abruptly and half ran, half stumbled from the room. He stood, chest heaving, against the wall in the corridor outside. "It's not her," he said as Devorkian approached. "It's not her, but it's . . . it's horrible."

"Yes, it is, Mr. Drummond. It is horrible. I'm sorry we had to put you through that. Are you sure it is not your wife?"

"Yes. Positive."

Devorkian looked at Drummond thoughtfully. He toyed with asking him for permission to search his house for fingerprints to prove the assertion definitively—for Drummond's "peace of mind." Then he thought again. Searching with Drummond's permission would mean a quick visit, not the thorough search he wanted to do. Without a search warrant, any evidence he found there—including the gun he hoped to find—might later be ruled inadmissible in court. And the very act of asking would give Drummond a warning. Drummond could just say no, and by the time Devorkian arranged for a search warrant, the gun would be long gone.

"Well, then," Devorkian said, "thank you, Mr. Drummond."

In his office, John Smyth hunched over his desk. The fluorescent lights droned, and the air conditioner whined inadequately against the Winnipeg summer. His suit coat hung down crookedly over his chair back, as if a great weight was attached to one arm. His desk and the floor were covered with piles of papers, leaving only the two-square-foot section of space in front of him, where he was working.

Smyth sighed deeply over the report in front of him. It was disturbing. Taken from the Evangelical Press News Service, it presented detailed statistics on sexual abuse by pastors and priests in the U.S.

Printing such news was one part of his job that Smyth hated, but he had not hesitated when deciding to put the report in *Grace* magazine. He had been one of the church magazine editors who had taken the lead in publishing such stories. "Sin needs to be exposed," he often said.

In one or two cases, in fact, Smyth himself had done some investigative reporting, exposing abusers in his own denomination. There had not been many, only twelve pastors altogether that he knew of, widely scattered in places and times. Out of well over a thousand pastors in five hundred churches in his denomination, that was statistically not very significant—about 1 percent. But for the victims, of course, it was very significant. And each one of these cases, in his denomination and others, had far-reaching implications, sending out ripples of evil in many directions.

One of those ripples was the widespread distrust sexual abuse created. For many people outside the church, such incidents reinforced their prejudice that all religious leaders were hypocritical and even dangerous, to the point that these people were afraid even to talk to a pastor. They created distrust inside the church too, an atmosphere of suspicion. From time to time, Smyth found he was harboring suspicions in the back of his mind, wondering whether the people he worked with could have guilty secrets. Could Clint Granowski or Harry Collins or Carl Brager have abused their church members or found ways to steal money from the church or even killed someone?

There were much stricter accountability procedures now, of course. But denominational leaders were human, not all-knowing like God; they could miss something. Or they could be guilty too. Perhaps most disconcerting of all, Smyth suspected that other church leaders might sometimes wonder about him too. . . .

His thoughts were interrupted by the *breeeap* of his telephone. Smyth jumped involuntarily.

"John?" a voice chirped into his ear. "It's Harry Collins!"

"Harry, how are you?"

"Oh, good, good. Better than many of my clients, I suppose."

"Things not going well on Main Street?"

"Things rarely go well on Main Street. You know that, John."

They chatted for a few minutes, but Smyth was starting to get the impression that Harry Collins had not yet said anything about the real reason he called.

"Harry, it's good talking . . . uh . . . Is this why you phoned?"

There was a pause. "Actually, I wanted to ask you a favor."

"Sure. Go ahead."

"There's this prostitute that we'd been working with. . . . That doesn't sound right. I mean, we had been relating to her."

"I hope these relations weren't sexual."

Harry was clearly flustered now. "No, no. Talking to her. We had been talking to her. You know we go out and try to become friends with the street people, the winos and the prostitutes."

"Yes, Harry. I know."

"This one in particular—we had talked a few times. She wouldn't say much about herself. Not many of them do."

"Yes."

"Well, she's disappeared. . . ."

"What do you mean, disappeared?"

"She just hasn't been around for a while. I even asked around. No one has seen her for a while."

"So she got off the street. But what do you want me to do, start a 'Personals' column so you can advertise for her? I don't think any of our readers would know her, Harry. At least, I hope not."

"No, no. It's just . . . well, she's been missing about four weeks. And her name is Grace."

John Smyth had stopped breathing. Finally, he gulped. "Oh," was all he could say.

"You see why I phoned you."

"What's the rest of her name? Grace who?"

"I don't know. She just went by the one name. A lot of prostitutes do. I don't even know if it was her real name."

"So, why *did* you phone me?"

"I wondered, you know, whether she could be the one you saw from the airplane."

"How did you know . . . ?"

"The pastors' prayer meeting, John."

"Of course."

"Do you think it could be her?"

"I don't know. This was in the backyard of a house, not downtown."

"Some guys take prostitutes home with them."

"And then kill them afterward?"

"Yeah. It happens."

"Yeah."

"Could it be her?"

"I don't know. I was up in the air. All I saw was this woman dressed in white, and . . ."

"White?" Harry interrupted.

"Yes, white. Why?"

"Grace always wore white. It was like a trademark. It went with the name Grace. Some of these girls make up identities —an image, almost like dressing up on Halloween. Grace wore white. It was one of the reasons I had hope for her. Most of the girls wear black or other dark colors. I sort of had the feeling she was . . . well . . . reaching out toward the light."

"Did she look like the police drawing in the paper?"

"Yeah, somewhat."

"You had better tell the police all this."

"Yes . . . uh . . . that's why I called you."

"What?"

"Well, since you saw it, after all. You're working with the police on this. They trust you."

"T-trust me?!" John Smyth stammered. How could he explain the questions the police were asking him—the unexpected visits, the demands for proof, the investigation of his personal life?

"Yes," Harry was continuing. "They know you. They will believe your evidence."

"But . . . but this is *your* evidence."

"Sure, but they will believe you on this."

"Why don't you tell them yourself?"

"Because I don't know the police. I don't get along too well with them. We're sort of on opposite sides."

"Opposite sides?"

"Yes. They're trying to arrest and punish people. I'm trying to redeem people. We sometimes get in each other's way."

"They also try to protect people—people like Grace."

"People like—no, not people like Grace. She was just a prostitute to them. But to me, she was, well, a human being, one of God's special creatures."

"So, what am I supposed to tell the police?"

"Just tell them what I told you. About Grace being missing and wearing white and all."

"But I'll have to tell them I heard it from you, and then they'll come to see you anyway."

"Yes, but it's still better if they hear it from you first. You're their buddy."

"Harry, I'm not their buddy. I'm not sure they even believe me about what I saw from the airplane."

"John, don't be hard on yourself. You're a very believable man. That's why the denomination made you editor."

"But . . ."

"Thanks, John. Just tell them about Grace. Maybe you can convince them to look for her. Let me know what they say."

"Harry . . ."

But Harry had hung up.

John Smyth spent fifteen minutes trying to figure out what he would say to Sergeant Prestwyck. He finally gave up and just dialed.

"RCMP. Constable Bisset speaking."

"Could I speak to Sergeant Prestwyck please?"

"I'm sorry. Sergeant Prestwyck is not available right now. Would you like to speak to another officer or leave a message?"

Smyth wasn't sure whether he was glad for the postponement or upset that he would have to worry about it longer. "No. Just ask him to call John Smyth."

"John Smith? What's your number?"

"He has my number."

"Yes, but why don't you give it to me anyway, just to be sure?"

John Smyth suspected he was being confused with an alias again. He gave the number.

"And what is this concerning?"

"Tell him it's about Grace."

"Grace? The woman who was murdered?"

"Yes. Just tell him it's John Smyth, the religious writer."

"Oh." Smyth could hear the tension drain out of Bisset's voice. "John *Smyth*."

Chapter 13

FRIDAY, JULY 12

At seven-forty-five Friday morning, John Smyth kissed Ruby good-bye and opened the front door. The wave of hot air that hit him told him that it was already hotter outside than inside. Winnipeg's winters are legendary for their cold, and its summers are known for their oppressive heat, at least by Canadian standards. He felt tired already.

He was halfway down the sidewalk before he noticed. Standing at the curb in front of his house was a familiar-looking blue car.

"Good morning, Mr. Smyth," Sergeant Prestwyck called through the open window.

"Good morning," John Smyth mumbled in reply.

"It's a warm day. Can I offer you a ride to work?"

Smyth smiled weakly and walked around to the passenger door. Before getting in, he waved to Ruby standing in the picture window.

They rode in silence for the first block as Smyth's anxiety

level rose. Finally, Prestwyck asked, "You called me yesterday? Decided to confess, have you?"

"Yes . . . No, I mean . . . You know, I'm getting a little tired of all this . . . insinuation. To suggest to my wife that I've been having affairs—"

Prestwyck leaned back in his seat and blew out his breath.

"Just doing my job, Mr. Smyth. In order to solve cases, we have to ask hard questions."

"Well, then ask *me* hard questions, but leave my family alone."

Prestwyck didn't answer, just drove. He pulled over in front of the denominational headquarters. "So why did you call?"

"Uh, a friend of mine asked me to pass some information on to you."

"A friend?"

"Yes. It's Harry Collins—he's administrator of the Grace Mission on Main Street. He relates to the downtown people—homeless, winos, and prostitutes. He thinks that one of the prostitutes he's talked to is missing. She goes by the name of Grace. And he says she looks something like the woman in the police drawing."

Prestwyck was silent a moment. "I see," he said, "and why did he tell you all this instead of telling the police?"

"He . . . since I told you about what I saw from the plane, he thinks that we're, uh, friends, that we're sort of working together."

Prestwyck's laughter was genuine but brief. "You told him what you saw from the plane?"

"Not directly. That is, I told the pastors' prayer fellowship, but he was . . ."

"The pastors' fellowship?"

"Yes. The pastors of the local Grace churches get together every other Thursday and pray together. Someone mentioned we should pray about the murder, and I said I might have seen it from the plane."

"You told them this last night?"

"No. A week ago."

"How many people were there?"

"I don't know—twelve or fifteen."

"Great. And how many people have they told by now?"

"I don't know. Things said at the prayer meetings are supposed to be confidential, although sometimes it doesn't matter; they're common knowledge."

"And some of these guys could have preached it to their whole congregations last Sunday?"

"I suppose, but I really don't think—"

"We don't need more publicity right now. Don't tell anyone else, okay?"

"Okay."

"And especially don't talk to reporters."

"Uh, okay."

"Does Harry Collins know he's going to have to talk to the police anyway?"

"Yes. He knows. I told him that. He's willing to talk."

"What else did he have to say?"

"Just that there was a prostitute he hadn't seen for some time, her name was Grace, and she always wore white."

"White?"

Smyth nodded.

"Is there anything else you have to tell me?"

"No," Smyth said weakly.

"Well . . ." Prestwyck gave a faint smile. "Stay in touch."

John Smyth got out of the car and walked in to work ten minutes early.

"Mrs. Crocker, I want to thank you for agreeing to come down here again."

It was ten in the morning, and Louise Crocker sat nervously in Devorkian's office, without Mary Alice this time.

"How many times did you see Mrs. Drummond?"

"I don't know. Fifty . . . hundreds. I mean, I often saw her in the yard or when she was walking to the store."

Devorkian smiled. Nosy neighbors were a great help in police work. "How many times did you see her closely, talk to her face-to-face?"

"Twenty, thirty?"

"Are you observant of people, Mrs. Crocker?"

"Yes, I think so. My husband says I am."

"Good. If I were to show you a woman's body, do you think you would be able to tell if it was Mrs. Drummond or not?"

Louise Crocker took a deep breath. This is what she had been expecting and fearing and, to be honest, hoping for too. Her life was not very exciting. "Yes," she said simply.

"Okay, but before you agree, I must warn you of something. The woman we found was outside for some time—weeks. There is a severe injury to the face and, well, it also looks as if a small animal chewed at the wound."

Louise sucked in her breath. "I—I still think I can do it," she said. "I mean, I should do it. I have a responsibility, don't I?"

"Thank you, Mrs. Crocker. Of course, it will make it harder for you to identify the woman, so feel free to tell me if you are not sure."

"I understand. Can . . . can I ask you something?"

"Yes."

"Why didn't you ask Mr. Drummond to identify the body?" She paused. "Oh. You don't trust him, do you?"

Devorkian knew he had to be careful. Who knew where Mary Alice Bruckner would take this line of thinking? "In a murder investigation, Mrs. Crocker, we can't afford to trust anybody. We just want to be sure, that's all."

"Did Mr. Drummond see the body? What did he say?"

"I'd rather not say, Mrs. Crocker. I'd rather you kept an open mind."

"Oh. That must be an awful way to live."

"What?"

"Never trusting anybody, I mean."

Devorkian had never thought about it like that before.

Prestwyck and Osnachuck stood in the living room of Grace Hutchinson's apartment, watching Leo Lazinski direct the RCMP forensics team.

"It's strange that we haven't found photos," Prestwyck said.

"There were pictures of two kids on the fridge."

"Yes, but no pictures of Grace Hutchinson."

"Do you think it means anything? Could the killer have taken the pictures so we couldn't identify the body?"

"Maybe. Or maybe all her old pictures were burned in a house fire or something. I don't think he would have taken the time to find every picture."

"Why not? He had two weeks. Maybe he was looking for something else."

"Robbery? I don't think so. Some of her jewelry and silver are still here. And would he have left the place neat? The maid said the place was already tidy when she got here."

"So, we've got a compulsively neat thief."

"Naw, I don't think so. This just doesn't *feel* like a robbery. At least, Lazinski said he's getting some good fingerprints."

"Probably the maid's."

"Yes, but he's getting some in drawers, on glasses in the kitchen cupboards, and so on. He's probably got Grace Hutchinson's, and it would be nice to find her killer's too, but I doubt it. If he's as careful as he seems, he'd wear gloves."

"We'll know when the reports come back."

Lazinski approached them. "You wanted to know if we found an address book. We found this at the back of a drawer." He handed over a small black book.

Prestwyck took it carefully. "It's been dusted for prints?"

"Yes, but there weren't any good ones, just a lot of smudges. It was dusty—probably an old one."

"Any sign of a purse?"

"No."

"No address book by the phone or anything?"

"A card with some professionals on it—doctor, dentist, mechanic, and so on. Doesn't look like any friends."

"And her phone is nonprogrammable, right?"

"No, it's programmable. It just doesn't have any programmed numbers on it."

"Redial?"

"The cleaning company. Evidently, the maid checked in after cleaning the place."

"Or the killer phoned for maid service. It figures. Bring me the card by the phone."

When Lazinski brought the card, Prestwyck handed it and the address book to Osnachuck. "Get onto these, will you?" he said.

"Yes, sir. Are you coming back to the office?"

"I'll drop you there. I'm going to do a little mission work."

"The religious guy's getting to you, eh?"

"In a manner of speaking. He's why I'm going there."

"Now, Mrs. Crocker, take a few deep breaths before we go in. This is not going to be pleasant."

Louise Crocker did so. She bestowed a quick half-smile on Devorkian, then he opened the door to the stainless steel room.

"Are you ready?" he asked when a stainless steel drawer had been pulled open. "Try not to look at the face, but at the whole body."

Louise nodded, and Devorkian pulled the sheet evenly back from the body. There were no tricks this time. Louise gasped and put her hand to her mouth. For a minute, she seemed to be struggling for breath, then she seemed to have gained control.

"Take your time. Look very carefully at the whole body," Devorkian advised.

At last, she turned away. Devorkian nodded to the morgue attendant and followed Louise from the room. She stood in the hall breathing deeply. She had taken it surprisingly well, Devorkian thought. She could make a good witness.

"Well?" he asked.

"I think it's her," Louise said. "I mean, she's the right size. The hair looks right—the right length at least—I know it's pretty messy. What I can see of the face, the eyes—it looks right."

"What about other things? The ears?"

"I don't know. I don't really remember Grace's ears."

"What about the hands? Were there any distinguishing marks?"

"The hands look right too—sort of average. Her fingers were neither long and thin nor short and stubby. She didn't have any birthmarks or anything like that that I know of. But you know it's really the face that we remember about people. And of course we can't see that now, can we?"

It was early afternoon, just past the lunchtime rush, when Sergeant Prestwyck walked into Grace Mission. He blinked, his eyes slowly adjusting to the dark and dingy interior. Bright windows were not common on Main Street, an area known more for broken glass than plate glass.

Harry Collins spotted him and rushed over. "Did you have to wear your uniform?" he said. "Come into my office. Your standing here is not good for business—drives away the customers."

Prestwyck smiled and followed Collins into the cubbyhole he called an office. "So you know why I'm here?" he asked.

"I presume it's about Grace," Harry replied. "You're John Smyth's friend."

Prestwyck smiled again. "I'm Sergeant Prestwyck," he said. "What do you have to tell me about Grace?"

What Harry Collins had to say was not much more than he had told John Smyth. The prostitute who called herself Grace had not been around for some time, three or four weeks probably. Harry had asked around a bit, but no one else seemed to have seen her either. Collins didn't know her that well. He had only talked to her four or five times. She had been on the street for a few months and had a room in one of the cheap hotels a couple of blocks down Main Street—he couldn't remember which one. He had seen the police drawing in the paper, and it looked as if it could be her, but even when Prestwyck handed him a larger, clearer copy, he couldn't be sure. It was only a drawing, not a photo, right? And he confirmed that she had been wearing white every time he saw her.

On his way back, Prestwyck stopped in at Winnipeg Police headquarters a few blocks farther south, just off Main Street. Devorkian smiled to see him. "It is a great day when we are honored with the presence of Her Majesty's Royal Horsemen in our humble establishment."

"Very funny," Prestwyck grumbled, slouching into a chair opposite Devorkian's desk.

"How's the investigation going, Sergeant?" Devorkian put a slight emphasis on *Sergeant,* implying that in the Winnipeg police force, at least, sergeant was a rank inferior to his own.

Prestwyck shrugged. "We searched Grace Hutchinson's apartment. She's definitely missing. We won't know for a little while whether fingerprints match or anything. Corporal Osnachuck is following up the other stuff, trying to trace friends and relatives. How's your end of the investigation?"

Devorkian paused and smiled again. "We're getting a warrant to search Gary Drummond's house. The neighbor gave a positive ID to the body." He was not very successful in keeping the gloat out of his face. Actually, he wasn't trying very hard.

"What about Drummond himself?"

"He denied it was her."

"You think a neighbor is a more reliable witness in identifying a woman's body than her husband is?"

"Drummond was very shaken up when he saw the body. I think he's lying."

"Then why would he come down in the first place?"

"Maybe he was afraid someone else would recognize his wife, and he came down to throw us off. It's happened before. Anyway, Drummond's the guy. I can feel it. Now I've just got to nail down the evidence."

Prestwyck shrugged. He seemed to be taking it quite well. "So you think you've solved my case, do you?"

"I don't know. It's too early to know for sure."

"So you probably don't want to know about the prostitute named Grace?"

Devorkian paled. "What prostitute?"

"A prostitute named Grace. She plies her trade not far from this very spot. Or she did. She's been missing for four weeks. Strange—one of your prostitutes is missing and you don't even know about it. Don't you keep track of what's going on in this city?"

"How did you find out about this? Her name's Grace?"

"Yes. She always wore white, too."

"Where did you get a lead on her?"

"Harry Collins from Grace Mission told me."

"Yes, we know Harry. Did he contact you?"

"Not exactly. Seems he's a friend of John Smyth."

"John Smyth? The religious guy?"

"I suspect Harry Collins is a religious guy too, seeing as how he runs Grace Mission. But then you know him better than we do." Prestwyck was clearly enjoying having the upper hand for a change.

"Have you checked this out?"

"Nope. I just came from Collins's office. And you're the one who needs to check it out. You and I are still working together on this investigation, right?"

"And the RCMP are too important to investigate murders of prostitutes?"

"No, Devorkian. The downtown is your beat; it's right outside your window. You're the guys with the street contacts; you have constables on patrol down here. You wanted this investigation, and as far as I'm concerned, you can have it. I'm sick of the whole mess."

"You're just going to dump it all in our lap? I guess if you can't handle it . . ."

"Devorkian, I don't care. We will follow up on Grace Hutchinson and keep looking for missing persons, looking for leads. Gary Drummond and the prostitute are your problems. I'm tired, and I'm going to take the weekend off. I'll talk to you again on Monday."

When he had left, Devorkian sighed. He was tired too, and he didn't need the extra complication of this new lead. Solving the murder of a middle-class housewife was one thing, but there was not much glory in solving the murder of a prostitute—nobody cared. On the other hand, it would still be good to solve an RCMP case. Devorkian smiled again, and called through the open door, "Hansson!"

Chapter 14

SATURDAY, JULY 13

A broad expanse of green lawn stretched out extravagantly in front of Manitoba's stately limestone Legislative Building, in sharp contrast to the dingy concrete of Main Street only a few blocks away. The poverty of inner-city neighborhoods is a traditional reality in Winnipeg, dating back to the immigrant slums of the late nineteenth century. Yet Winnipeg is also a city of numerous and magnificent parks. The city has responded to its challenges with a green weapon, its green parks and spacious lawns offering hope to rich and poor.

On this morning, a variety of people walked, wandered, sat, and lay on the grass in front of the Legislative Building. Scattered here and there were small knots of people, mostly women. The knots ebbed and flowed, stood still, eddied back into the current, and gradually converged toward the front steps of the Legislature. On the lower steps, three women and two men were in the final stages of setting up a sound system.

A few moments later, Mary Alice Bruckner stepped to the microphone. "Women will win!" she shouted into the microphone. It was the rallying cry for Women Against Risk, but it also served to call the demonstration together. The knots of women broke and flowed to the center of the lawn in front of the Legislature's steps.

"Women will win!" she repeated, and the crowd of women broke into a cheer. "Sisters," she continued, "we are at war. Men are still abusing, raping, and murdering our sisters and our daughters and our mothers. We cannot allow this to continue. It must be stopped, and we are the ones who must stop it. Women will win!"

The crowd cheered.

"We're here today," she continued, "because another woman has been brutally raped and murdered." Mary Alice took on a more somber tone. "You've read it in the papers. A woman has been found in the woods near Winnipeg, brutally beaten and murdered. Another innocent woman snatched from her home and tortured to satisfy the evil desires of men. Her name was Grace. She was everything her name implies—gracious, loving, kind, nurturing. And some man has murdered her! She was murdered four weeks ago, and the police haven't done a thing to find and punish the abuser. They didn't even find the body for two weeks."

The crowd moaned.

"Who are the police?" Mary Alice continued. "They are mostly men, and men don't want to stop other men who abuse women. But we will."

The crowd roared its approval.

Mary Alice became quieter again. "I want to tell you something. While the police were sitting around doing nothing, *we* have solved Grace's murder!"

The crowd gasped.

"One of our members recognized the dead woman's photo, and on Thursday she turned Grace Drummond's murdering husband in to the police. This courageous woman is here with us today—my cousin, Louise Crocker!"

The crowd applauded, a little uncertainly.

Louise Crocker was standing stock-still at the edge of the crowd, her mouth frozen open with surprise.

"Come up here, Louise," called Mary Alice.

Louise stumbled forward. Mary Alice pushed her toward the microphone. Louise hesitated, took a deep breath, and then told her story simply. Her neighbor was a nice, quiet woman. She had told Louise once that her husband had hit her. Then, about four weeks before, Grace had simply disappeared. When Louise saw the drawing in the paper, she had thought it looked like her neighbor, and she and Mary Alice had gone to the police. Yesterday, she had gone to the morgue and identified the body of Grace Drummond.

Sergeant Prestwyck was out of uniform. Wearing threadbare slippers, sweatpants with a hole in one knee, and a dingy white tee shirt, he relaxed in a beat-up recliner, sipping coffee from a chipped mug, and reading the Saturday paper. The phone rang, and he cursed.

"What do you want?" he barked into the receiver. He had picked it up on the twelfth ring.

"Sergeant Prestwyck, I hope I'm not disturbing you."

"Devorkian! What do you want? I told you I was taking the weekend off."

"I know," Devorkian replied in a serious voice, "but you're missing all the fun."

"What fun? Have you solved the case? Did Drummond confess?"

"No, I haven't solved the case, but Mary Alice Bruckner

has. I'm down at the Legislative Building. Women Against Risk is holding an anti–violence-against-women rally. They've just announced that the dead woman is Grace Drummond and that her husband murdered her."

Dead silence hung in the air. "You're kidding," Prestwyck finally managed. "That's libelous."

"It sure is. Pretty irresponsible too. But we're the ones who are going to have to pick up the pieces."

"We'll do it on Monday. I'm sure glad they haven't found out about Grace Hutchinson yet. Or Grace the prostitute."

"Don't count on it. They're on a roll. They'll probably make more accusations before long."

Prestwyck cursed again.

"Aren't you going to come down and join the fun?"

"I don't want to get within twenty miles of that woman. I'll talk to you on Monday. Thanks for ruining my weekend."

Devorkian managed to get his ear away from the phone quickly enough to avoid the deafening crash of the receiver at the other end. "I wonder if he broke his phone," he muttered as he wandered across the green lawn to join the uniformed constable on duty.

On the Legislature steps, a new speaker was at the microphone.

"Who's that?" Devorkian asked Constable Martin, who worked the downtown beat.

"Vicki Alloran. She's head of the WWSW."

"WWSW? What's that? Women's Worldwide Sumo Wrestling?"

"Women With Street Workers. It's an advocacy group for prostitutes."

"I don't know about the woman Mary Alice and Louise were talking about," Alloran was saying, "but there are many abused women in this city. Many of them live on the streets near here. I know. I work with them. They have suffered the worst possible abuses at home. They have been raped and beaten and verbally abused by their fathers and grandfathers and brothers and boyfriends. They have fled to the streets of downtown Winnipeg, where they run the risk of being raped, beaten, robbed, strung out on drugs, and murdered.

"I'm not saying Mary Alice and Louise are wrong. But I want to talk to you about another Grace who is missing. She's a young girl who has been on the street here for the past several months. She had no last name because she did not want to be named for any of those evil men who had driven her out onto the streets. But she always wore white. I see that as a symbol of the pure, innocent girl underneath all of the abuse and suffering, a little girl dressed in white, crying to get out of the cruel prison that men had put her in. Grace has been missing for four weeks.

"Do the police care? Does the government care? Does anyone care? If the police are not doing anything to solve the murder of a married woman, they are certainly not going to do anything for the Graces of Main Street. If they are not going to do anything, who will? It is up to us, you and me, to bring change, to achieve justice for the abused women of this world."

For a moment, Devorkian found himself moved by the woman's earnest eloquence. Then he was distracted by a movement to his right. A ragged man had come up to Constable Martin and was standing in front of him. His jaw worked as if he was trying to say something.

"What?" Martin demanded.

"You—you're a policeman?" the man said.

"Yes."

"I want to tell you. . . . I know her. . . . She is the one."

Martin seemed ready to chase the man away, but Devorkian put a hand on his arm. He turned to the man. "I am Detective Devorkian of the Winnipeg Police Department. Do you know something about the dead woman we found a couple of weeks ago?"

The man nodded solemnly. "Grace," he said.

"Would you like to go somewhere and talk about this? Are you hungry? We could go to a coffee shop."

The man looked horrified.

Martin whispered to Devorkian, "Don't. It could be dangerous for him to be seen eating with a policeman."

Devorkian nodded. "Would you rather talk here?"

The man nodded.

Devorkian asked, "What's your name?"

The horrified look returned, but it was driven from his face by a determined look. "David. David Mackenzie."

"And you live near Main Street?"

David looked grateful for the vagueness of the question. He nodded.

"Do you know the woman who was murdered?"

David looked confused. Devorkian rephrased the question. "You know something. Why don't you just tell me what it is you know."

David struggled for a few moments. "Her name is Grace," he said at last.

"The woman you know about?"

David nodded. "She lives at the Queen's."

"The Queen's?"

"Probably the Queen's Hotel," Martin put in.

David nodded again.

"She worked as a prostitute, didn't she, David?"

"Sometimes."

"Where?"

"Usually by the Queen's, sometimes the next street over."

"What else do you have to tell me?"

"I looked and I looked, and she's gone."

"She's missing? For how long?"

Time was clearly not one of David's strong points. "Don't know. Month, maybe. Weeks."

"Do you know what happened to her?"

David shook his head.

"Can you remember anything different about the time she disappeared?"

David appeared to ponder for a while, then shook his head again. "But I seen her in the paper."

"You mean this woman?" Devorkian pulled a flyer from his pocket.

The paper shook as David held it. "That's her. She always wore white. She was an angel. She talked to me."

"What did she say?"

"Nothing. Just hi. Once she said, 'Good morning'."

"Anything else at all? Think. Anything about her past?"

David shook his head sadly.

"What was her last name?"

David was still shaking his head sadly. "Don't know. Just Grace. The angel in white." David smiled crookedly. "I called her *that*."

"What else can you tell us?"

David shook his head again. "I had to tell . . ."

"David, did you do anything to Grace? Did you kill her?"

The horrified look returned. He shook his head violently. For a second, Devorkian had the strange impression the man's head might shake too violently and fall right off his neck. "No, David, I don't believe you did. But you did see her after she died, didn't you?"

There was more shaking. "Only in the paper."

"Did you see who took her away?"

"No." David choked back a sob. "I wish I done . . ."

"David," Devorkian said, "I do believe you didn't kill Grace. Now, listen. We are going to try to find out if the dead woman we found is really your Grace. And we are going to try to find out who killed her and punish that person, okay? Now, if you find out anything else, will you find a police officer and tell him immediately?"

David nodded.

"And David, if I find out who killed Grace, I would like to tell you. How can I find you?"

"Leave a message at Grace?"

"But Grace is dead, David."

"I think he means the Grace Mission," Martin put in.

"Is that it, David? I should leave a message for you at the Grace Mission?"

David nodded. "Or Stetson's," he blurted.

Martin put a hand on Devorkian's arm. "It's okay."

"Thank you, David. I think you may have really helped Grace."

But David was already gliding away in the direction of Main Street. He moved with surprising speed for a man who hardly seemed to be moving his feet.

"What did he mean by Stetson's?" Devorkian asked Constable Martin when the scruffy man had disappeared.

"The alley behind the Stetson's leather store. I suspect he lives there. That is quite an admission for him to make. He must really want to do something for Grace."

"So you're inclined to believe him?"

"Yes."

"Maybe he just heard all the speeches and they put the idea into his head."

"No," Martin said. "I don't think he heard the speeches.

Guys like David don't notice too much around them, especially if it's outside their experience. They can spot a cigarette butt at fifty paces, but they would probably sleep through a parade marching down their alley."

"And yet he noticed Grace," Devorkian mused. "I wonder what that could mean."

Chapter 15

MONDAY, JULY 15

Sergeant Prestwyck was true to his word and, in spite of the late-breaking exposé of his case, took the whole weekend off. Scott Ledyear did not. The story of the missing woman had elevated him to front-page status on the paper, and he was taking full advantage of it. His full account of the Women Against Risk rally took half of the front page in the Sunday paper and all of page four, with the promise of more details to come.

Detective Devorkian and the Winnipeg Police were not idle, either. They had spent much of the weekend trying to get more information on Grace Drummond and Grace-the-prostitute-in-white. By Monday, however, their investigations had advanced scarcely more than Prestwyck's had.

By eight-thirty that morning, Prestwyck had already left three messages for Devorkian, but Devorkian was occupied elsewhere.

The early morning sun made Gary Drummond's old black Cadillac shine like silk—and pushed the edges of his scowl toward a semblance of a small smile. One of the advantages of being a mechanic was the deals you could find. When you came across a vintage car at the right price, you knew if it was in good running condition or not. And this particular automobile had been a true steal.

He reached for the door handle but then jumped back as if it were red hot. It was not the car that had shocked him, but the voice behind him. He immediately recognized Devorkian's even tones.

"Good morning, Mr. Drummond."

"What are you doing here?"

"We have been doing some thinking about what you told us the other day. We realize that the body we found was hard to recognize since the face was so mangled. We were wondering if you would allow us to search your house."

"What for?" Drummond asked tensely.

"For fingerprints mainly, so we can see if your wife's fingerprints match the dead woman's."

"I told you it wasn't her. I should know. I'm her husband, ain't I?"

"Mr. Drummond, anyone can make a mistake, especially under the circumstances. Now if you'll just—"

"No." Drummond's voice had been steadily rising. "I know what you're trying to do. You're trying to blame me for murdering that woman. You're being bulldozed by those loony broads down at the Legislature! I tell you that dead woman is not my wife!"

"I'm sorry you're taking that attitude, Mr. Drummond. I'm afraid we're going to have to search your house anyway." Devorkian held out a piece of paper. "We have a search warrant."

"You _____ !" Drummond shouted. "You're trying to frame

me!" He swung his big fist in the direction of Devorkian's face.

Fortunately—or unfortunately, depending on one's point of view—a constable stepped in front of Devorkian at that moment and took the full force of Drummond's punch on the left cheekbone. Other officers quickly jumped on Drummond, who struggled wildly to throw them off. His face was pushed into the ground beside his shiny Cadillac, cuffs were clamped onto his wrists, and he went limp. He began to sob softly.

The search proceeded carefully, room by room, while Drummond sat silently on the living-room sofa. The phone rang.

"That's probably my boss," Drummond said suddenly. "He'll fire me if I don't come in to work."

"Don't worry, Mr. Drummond," Devorkian said. "I'll answer it." He picked up the receiver and said a low, clipped "Hello" into the receiver.

"Detective Devorkian?" came over the phone from the other end.

"Yes?"

"This is Constable Hansson. I'm sorry—"

"What do you mean phoning me on Drummond's phone? What if we weren't inside yet?"

"I'm sorry, sir, but you weren't answering on your cell or the car radios. I thought I should reach you right away. Sergeant Prestwyck of the RCMP has phoned for you three times already."

"What does he want?"

"The first two times, he just asked you to call him back. The third time, he left a message. It says: "Press conference at ten-thirty, RCMP headquarters."

"What?!"

When he had hung up, Drummond asked for permission to phone his boss, but Devorkian was already punching numbers.

"What do you mean calling a joint press conference without consulting me?" he demanded of Sergeant Prestwyck.

"I tried to consult you. It's not my fault you come in to work late."

"I'm not late. I'm out investigating your case. I can't come over and talk with the press now."

"Suit yourself. I've called a press conference. If the Winnipeg police don't want to be present, that's okay with me."

"What are you going to tell them? We're the ones digging out the facts."

"If you don't come, I guess you won't know what I'll tell them—at least, until the papers come out."

"Look, I'm in the middle of something. We're searching Drummond's house. Can't you postpone the press conference till this afternoon?"

"No. I'll hold off until eleven. I can't wait much longer if we want to make the six o'clock news. Don't you think we should say something in response to the rally on Saturday?"

"Yes, but we should have said something yesterday. You did nothing all weekend. Why are you rushing now?"

"Because I decided it was time. This is my investigation, remember? Now, do you want to take part or not?"

Devorkian slammed down the phone.

At ten minutes to eleven, Devorkian marched into Prestwyck's office. The search was almost finished, and he had calmed down somewhat. "What are you going to tell the press?" he demanded.

Prestwyck frowned. "We're going to have to try to get out of this mess we're in. I think we have to tell the press about the three missing women—Grace Hutchinson, Grace Drummond, and Grace the prostitute—and drive it through the press's thick skulls that we are still investigating. This is precisely why I didn't want to release details about the dead woman. It gets a lot of people all worried about perfectly innocent people who aren't even involved."

"I have never met one of those."

"What?"

"A perfectly innocent person."

Prestwyck regarded him thoughtfully. "You know, I'd bet you and that religious writer have more in common than you think."

"What are you talking about?"

"That's what the preachers say, eh? That everybody's a sinner? So you must have a bit of the preacher in you, too."

Devorkian snorted. "God forbid."

"Anyway, you know what I mean about the press."

"Yes, but the publicity did get us three good possibilities for Grace's identity."

"Huh. I wonder what we'll get out of this press conference?"

"Ulcers, most likely. I just hope that Mary Alice Bruckner isn't there."

Reporters had been waiting impatiently for forty-five minutes by the time the two policemen walked in. Prestwyck looked around but could see no sign of Mary Alice Bruckner. He wondered if she had realized she had gone too far at the rally on Saturday and was keeping a low profile. He doubted it. It was more likely that, since he had called the press conference at short notice, she hadn't found out about it in time. They sat at a long table, and Prestwyck pulled a microphone toward him.

"We want to update you on the progress of our investigation of the woman's body found July 1 east of Winnipeg," Prestwyck said. "As we reported some time ago, the police have reason to believe the woman's name may have been Grace. We understand that at a rally at the Legislative Building on Saturday, statements were made that the dead woman may be either a woman named Grace Drummond or another woman, a prostitute named Grace, no surname given. The police believe that such statements are premature and irresponsible. At this point, we have no direct evidence that either of these two may be the dead woman. The investigation by the RCMP and Winnipeg Police is ongoing.

"We are currently seeking information as to the whereabouts of three women named Grace. One is Grace Drummond of 439 Mapleleaf Street. The second is the suspected prostitute named Grace who frequently dressed in white and who lived in the downtown core. The third is a Grace Hutchinson of the Livingstone Apartments, 1147 Porter Avenue number 307. Let me emphasize that none of these women is officially listed as missing, and there is no direct evidence that any of them is even connected with the dead woman. However, the police would appreciate the assistance of the public in locating these women as well as identifying the dead woman. If any of the public recognize her from the police drawing, they should immediately contact either the RCMP or the Winnipeg police. Detective Devorkian of the Winnipeg Police Department is with us today. We will be willing to answer a few questions at this time."

Scott Ledyear was the first to his feet. "Why do you say you haven't identified the dead woman when her body has been positively identified by Louise Crocker as Grace Drummond?"

"Due to the condition of the body, identification is difficult," Devorkian replied. "We have not confirmed Mrs. Crocker's tentative identification."

"Do you believe Ms. Crocker is lying?"

"No," Devorkian stated. "We believe she may be mistaken. Her identification was only a tentative one."

"Why are the police unwilling to believe female witnesses? Do you believe they are less reliable than male witnesses?"

"No," Devorkian stated. "The police take seriously the evidence of all witnesses. There is no bias among the police."

"Are you sure that isn't Mary Alice Bruckner in disguise?" Prestwyck whispered to Devorkian. Devorkian smiled.

"If there is no bias, why are women still a minority in the police force?" Ledyear continued.

"You will have to ask that question of the police chief or the Police Commission."

"Why has it taken weeks to even identify the body? If it was a man who was murdered, would the police have taken this more seriously?"

Prestwyck answered this time. "Believe me, Mr. Ledyear, the police have been taking this matter very seriously."

Another reporter jumped to his feet. "Why have the police not investigated the disappearance of the prostitute named Grace?"

"We only learned on Friday that she may be missing," Prestwyck said. "The Winnipeg Police are investigating that matter as we speak."

"Why are the police so slow to investigate crimes against prostitutes? Do the police consider that prostitutes deserve to be murdered?"

And so it went for half an hour. Prestwyck finally called an end to the press conference with the words, "The police would love to spend the whole day talking to the press, but this is keeping us from our investigations."

"Want some lunch?" Prestwyck asked as they were leaving the room. "We need to talk."

Devorkian nodded absently, his mind still on the press conference.

"I'll order in," Prestwyck added. "I doubt if any restaurant in the city would be safe from those guys."

Prestwyck swallowed a mouthful of hamburger and asked, "Okay, where are we? Is Drummond really the guy?"

"I don't know. My team is still at his house, and I want to talk to him again."

"What about the prostitute?"

"We received another report on Saturday about her being missing."

"From Women With Street Workers?"

"From them, but there was another report as well, from a wino named David Mackenzie. He came up to us and volunteered information while we were at the rally."

"A bit unusual."

"Yes. I'm inclined to believe him."

"What did he say?"

"That's the bad news. He said nothing new, just that she was missing. How's the investigation of Grace Hutchinson going?"

"We searched the apartment, haven't traced her yet. I'll get the lab report this afternoon. She wrote out a check for the July rent but left it in her own apartment—never gave it to the apartment manager."

The two men sat in silence for a while. Neither was willing to give further details of his own investigations.

"Three Graces," Devorkian mused. "Weren't there three Graces in Greek mythology?"

"How should I know? Ask John Smyth. He's the writer."

"Ah, yes. How is Mr. Smyth?"

"I'm still pushing him. He's rattled, but I haven't gotten anything more yet. Tell you the truth, I don't really think—"

"Now I remember. There were three Graces: Aglaia, who gave away, Euphrosyne, who received, and . . . somebody else, who gave back."

"How do you know all that?"

"The Winnipeg police have an advantage over the RCMP. We've been to school."

Prestwyck glared at Devorkian. "Well, it doesn't help us, does it? We have three possible murder victims, all named Grace, and none of them is giving us anything. Which one do you suppose it will be?"

"Ah, that is the question. Which one?" But Devorkian thought he knew.

It was one-thirty by the time Devorkian got back to Winnipeg Police headquarters. Mike Hosschuk was waiting in his office, his stocky body slumped in the fake-leather side chair, his eyes at half-mast. He straightened when Devorkian walked in. Devorkian smiled slightly. He'd always envied the sergeant's catlike ability to relax totally one moment, then spring into total alertness the next.

"How was the press conference?" Hosschuk asked.

"Awful. What did you find?"

"Lots of prints. I don't think the place has been cleaned in weeks."

"Of course not. His wife has been gone for four weeks, remember? Have you fingerprinted Drummond?"

"Yes. We're getting ready to charge him with resisting arrest and assaulting an officer, but we haven't done it yet."

"Good. We'll hold off on that. I want to stretch it out and keep him around as long as possible. Is he here?"

"Yes, in a holding cell."

"Did he want a lawyer?"

"No. He didn't want one."

"Are you sure?"

"Got it on tape."

"Good man. What else did you find?"

"No blood that we could see. There's a fist-sized hole in the plaster. I asked him how it got there, and he says he did it—after she left."

"Nothing else?"

"Just this." Hosschuk held up a plastic bag with a silver object in it. Devorkian's eyes widened. "It's a forty-four. It was in a closet. No permit. Thought you'd like to see it before I sent it down to forensics."

"You're right about that."

"So, what next?"

"I think it's time we talked to Mr. Drummond."

"Good afternoon, Mr. Drummond," Devorkian said as he walked into the room. "How are you doing?"

Drummond glared sullenly at Devorkian.

"Mr. Drummond, your wife left you on Sunday, the sixteenth of June. Is that right?"

"Yeah . . . well, early that morning."

"And did she have a reason to leave you?"

"I already told you that. We had a fight the night before."

"What about?"

"Nothing. It don't matter. She just left."

"But why did she leave, Mr. Drummond?" Devorkian had moved his face close to Drummond's.

"Don't matter."

"It *does* matter, Mr. Drummond. Why would she leave? Maybe she didn't leave. Maybe you shot her with this." Devorkian shoved the plastic bag with its silver contents into Drummond's face.

"No . . ."

"Yes, Mr. Drummond. You shot her, didn't you?"

"No!"

"Yes! You took this gun and shot her."

"No . . . I—"

"This is your gun, isn't it, Mr. Drummond?"

"I—I don't know. I have one like that."

"Why do you have a gun, Mr. Drummond?"

"I . . . for protection . . . I used to work as night watchman sometimes at the shop."

"Did you have a license to carry a gun as a security guard?"

Drummond hung his head and said nothing.

"Have you ever shot this gun, Gary?"

"A couple of times, practicing."

"And a couple of times into Grace's face?"

"No. I told you. She went away."

"Why would she go away? I don't believe she just went away. I don't believe she had a reason to. What did you argue about?"

"Nothing."

"Don't be stupid, Gary. She wouldn't go away and stay away for a month just because she burnt the toast. What did you argue about?"

"Nothing. I—"

"She didn't have a reason to leave, did she?"

"Yes! We argued—"

"What about?"

"I—I lost my temper. We argued—"

"What about!?"

"We . . . uh . . . we argued because she wasn't getting

pregnant. The doctor says there's a chance she could get pregnant, and I said she wasn't trying hard enough. She didn't want to . . . uh, you know . . . that night."

"You mean she didn't want to make love to you? Mr. Drummond, were you drunk?"

"No . . . uh, I had had a couple of drinks, but I wasn't really—"

"Did you hit her?"

"No."

"What? Not at all? Weren't you angry?"

"Yeah, but I didn't . . . I—"

"What did you do? Push her?"

"Yeah."

"How many times?"

"Just a couple."

"A couple of times? Or was it three or four or five?"

"Two or three maybe . . . not five."

"A couple of shoves and then you hit her, right?" Devorkian was now standing over Drummond, leaning into his face. In the back of his mind the idea flickered momentarily that Mary Alice Bruckner might have more respect for police efforts to solve crimes against women if she could hear him now.

"No, I never hit her . . . Not then . . ."

"Not then? What? You hit her later?"

"Not later . . . earlier."

"Earlier? But you said you didn't hit her. You lied!"

"No, not then. Not that night. I hit her once, earlier, six months ago."

"Once. Nobody hits his wife just once, Gary."

"I did. It scared me. I never did again. I went for walks."

"Walks?"

"Yeah. After that, when I got mad, I went for a walk so I wouldn't hit her. That's what I did that night."

"When? Before or after you hit her?"

"I told you. I didn't hit her."

"Before or after you killed her?"

"Killed her? I didn't kill her. I didn't even hit her, just pushed her. And then I went for a walk, a long walk."

"Where?"

"Just around."

"Around to a bar?"

Drummond paused. "Yeah. I guess."

"What time did you get home?"

"About one."

"One o'clock in the morning? And your wife was gone?"

"No, but she was in bed. I slept in the spare room. We were going to use it for a nursery if . . ."

"How do you know your wife was in bed?"

"I listened at the bedroom door. I could hear her breathing."

"So you got angry, went out and got drunk, and then came back and just went to bed?"

"Yeah."

"No, Gary, you didn't go to bed. You were drunk; you were mad. You got your gun and you killed her, right?"

"No! She was alive. I'm not like that when I'm drunk. I just get sort of sad. I was tired. I went to bed. When I got up, she was gone."

"Gone? What do you mean gone?"

"Just . . . gone. It was after ten in the morning when I woke up, and a bunch of her stuff was gone . . . and her car." He looked up at Devorkian. "She drives this little Sable. I just gave it a tune-up."

"Where did she go? To her parents? To a shelter?"

"I don't think so. That's not what she said."

"So you did talk to her that morning?"

"No. Not then. The night before."

"What did she say?"

"I've told you that. She said she was going to Johnny Cockerill."

"Who's Johnny Cockerill?"

"I've told you that, too. I think he's an old boyfriend. She only started talking about him the past few weeks. She said . . . she said he was man enough to get her pregnant. That's when I pushed her."

Gary Drummond was sitting quietly now, his head down, drained. Devorkian wasn't sure where to take the interrogation next.

Chapter 16

TUESDAY, JULY 16

Good morning, Prestwyck. Seen the paper?"

"What are you laughing at, Devorkian? That idiot is slandering you too." The newspaper lay on Prestwyck's desk, its headline blaring: "Cops 2 steps behind."

"Well," Devorkian said, "I guess if you're one step, I'm the other."

Scott Ledyear had been in particularly fine form on page one with an account comparing yesterday's press conference to Saturday's rally, clearly insinuating that the police were incompetent. The editorial on the op-ed page turned insinuation into more direct insult: "The RCMP and the Winnipeg Police held a press conference Monday morning," the copy read, "to announce what the general public apparently knew two days earlier." The account went on to describe the "three missing women" and repeated many of the allegations made at the Women Against Risk rally. The police were not even given credit for finding out about Grace Hutchinson: "The police were informed about the third missing woman by another woman, apartment manager Gladys Plumtre." In an aside that foreshadowed Scott Ledyear's theme for tomorrow, the editor wondered, "Are there really three missing or murdered women? Can't the police find anyone?"

The editorial concluded, "The investigation has resulted in unprecedented cooperation between the RCMP and the Winnipeg Police, but it doesn't seem to be working. The police are making little progress. They started off investigating one missing woman, and now there are three."

"You know, I haven't seen much of this 'unprecedented cooperation,'" Prestwyck barked into the phone. "You're not telling me anything. What's going on? What have you found out?"

"We're charging Gary Drummond today." Devorkian paused. "With assaulting an officer."

"So you really don't know anything."

"Not much. We haven't got the results from the search yet. What have you got on Grace Hutchinson?"

"Don't know yet."

"Your people are having trouble keeping up, are they?"

"I'll have the report this morning."

"And it's going to say nothing, right?"

"Hey, listen, you—!"

"Can't listen now, Sergeant Prestwyck, I've got places to go." The line went dead as Devorkian hung up. Prestwyck glared at the receiver for a long minute, before slamming it down on his end.

"Osnachuck!" he yelled.

"Here it is," Osnachuck said, hurrying into Prestwyck's office.

"You got the report? Good. What's it say?"

"I just got it from Lazinski. I haven't read all of it—"

"Give me the high points."

"They . . . uh . . . they didn't find any prints that matched in Hutchinson's apartment."

"Are you sure?"

"Yeah, I'm sure. That's what took so long. They went over every print twice. Nothing."

"But the woman's still missing."

Osnachuck shrugged.

"What about the envelope addressed to the apartment manager?"

"It contained a check for the rent, no explanatory note."

"And the phone numbers?"

"Her dentist took Monday off. I reached him at home last night. He said he'll pick up her records at his office and meet me at the morgue at eight-thirty."

"What about the other numbers?"

"Nothing yet. I'm still working on them. Do you want to come with me to the morgue?"

"No," Prestwyck growled. "You work on those other numbers. I'll go to the morgue."

The police cars pulled up in front of a grubby five-story building on Main Street. Two officers hurried to the back of the building to watch the rear exits. Devorkian led a parade of officers through the front door of the building and into a dingy, dimly lit lobby. The room smelled, not of urine or beer or smoke or body odor or dust, but of an indistinguishable combination that gave an overwhelming impression of decay. The officers spread around the room. A shuffling noise was heard; a dark figure lurched into view in a doorway behind the counter and froze. He was a dirty, unshaven man in a stained blue tee shirt. A ragged mustache hung over his lips, and his sparse hair poked out at odd angles. His right hand, caught in the act of rubbing his eye, seemed glued to his forehead.

"Good morning, Bill," Constable Martin said.

The man in the doorway jumped slightly but remained where he was. His eyes darted sharply around the room from one unsmiling face to another.

"Come to the counter, Bill," Martin said.

The man shook himself, dropped his hand, and shuffled toward the counter.

"Bill Cocker," Martin said.

Devorkian stepped forward to the counter. "Good morning, Mr. Cocker." He smiled. "We're looking for one of the guests in this hotel. Woman named Grace. A prostitute."

"I don't know nothing about what people staying here do for a living. Don't have nothing to do with that. I just rent the rooms. I'm clean."

Devorkian looked hard at the clerk. He obviously hadn't meant that last remark literally. "Yes, Mr. Cocker, but the woman named Grace does have a room here?"

"No . . . uh . . . yeah, she did. But she's not here any more."

"I know that, Mr. Cocker. But she *did* have a room here?"

"Yeah."

"What was her full name?"

"She . . . uh . . . she didn't have one. She didn't give one."

"What did she sign in the register?"

"I told you. Grace."

"Just Grace? Hand me the register, Mr. Cocker."

Cocker didn't move. "At first, she didn't give a last name, just wrote Grace. I asked her for a full name. Then she wrote Grace White."

"The register, Mr. Cocker."

Cocker pulled a well-thumbed book from under the counter. He opened it, flipped through a few pages, then turned the book to face Devorkian. "There it is, Grace White."

"So she arrived in February, has been here three or four months. Room 308."

"Yeah."

"Did she show you any ID?"

"No. I didn't ask."

"Why not?"

Cocker shrugged, his jaw worked, but no words came out.

"How did she pay?"

"Cash."

"Did she always pay cash?"

"Yeah, every week, regular."

"And she always stayed in the same room? Or did she change rooms?"

"No, she was always in 308. She asked once for a second floor room to be easier for the johns so they wouldn't . . . so she, uh, would be closer to the john."

"Didn't her room have a bathroom, Mr. Cocker?"

"Yeah."

"So you did know she was a prostitute?"

"No . . . I suspected . . . didn't have no proof. I can't keep hookers out without proof or I get in trouble."

"How much extra did she pay for her rent?"

"Just a hundred bucks a week, like it says in the register."

"How much?"

"Just a hundred bucks."

"Do you know what the penalty is for running a house of prostitution, Mr. Cocker?"

"No. I . . ."

"Look, I don't care about you, Mr. Cocker. I just want to know about Grace. How much extra?"

"Another hundred."

"Does the hotel owner know about this, Mr. Cocker?"

Cocker shook his head.

"Just a hundred bucks? That's not much, not much for a pimp." Devorkian pressed harder now, deliberately switching to the man's first name. "Were you her pimp, Bill?"

Cocker shook his head more vehemently, his eyes suddenly big. "No . . . no . . . If the pimps found out, they'd get me. You can't . . ."

"How much, Bill?"

"Just a hundred, I swear it—plus an extra twenty if I sent someone up. But I didn't do it very much. Too risky. What if it was a pimp?"

"Did Grace have a pimp, Bill?"

"No, I don't think so. No."

"Was she on drugs?"

"No . . . I don't know. I don't think so."

"Bill, was she on drugs?"

"No. She didn't act like it."

"Then why was she working as a prostitute, Bill?"

"I don't know. She didn't talk much."

"Did you see this picture in the paper, Bill?"

Cocker seemed startled by the change in direction—as he was intended to be. "No . . . Yes . . . Yes, I seen it."

"Is this the Grace who was staying here, Bill?"

"I don't know. It don't exactly look right. It could be. It's only a drawing. Heck, old John can draw better than that when he's not too drunk, and you can't always tell who that's supposed to be."

"Why didn't you phone the police when you saw Grace's picture in the paper, Bill?"

"Like I said, it didn't look that much like her. There's a lot of women who look like that."

"A lot of women named Grace?"

Cocker didn't know what to say.

"We will keep this," Devorkian said, picking up the register.

Seeing Cocker about to protest, he added, "You can get a new register, can't you, Bill, with the extra money you got from Grace?"

Cocker leaned back, away from the counter.

Devorkian handed the book to Sergeant Hosschuk. He pulled a document from his jacket pocket. "Do you know what this is?"

Cocker shook his head unconvincingly.

"It's a search warrant for Grace White's room—308."

"You knew already?"

"Yes."

"But she's not there."

"We know that, Bill."

"But she's . . . I rented the room."

"What?"

"I rented the room . . . to someone else. Well, she was gone, she wasn't paying no more. I couldn't let it stay empty. Owner doesn't like—"

"So you knew she was gone for good. Did she take her things?"

"No."

"When did she leave?"

"I don't know, a month ago. It was a Saturday night. She'd just paid the rent for the next week. But she wasn't here Sunday. I never saw her again. So when the week was over, I rented the room to someone else."

"And she didn't take her things?"

"I told you. No."

"What happened to them?"

"I put them in a bag, a garbage bag. It's in the basement, I think. I put it there. There wasn't much. I was saving it for her, honest."

"Do you have your passkey, Bill? Good. Let's go up to

room 308, and then you can show Sergeant Hosschuk the bag in the basement. Don't worry. Constable Shaw will watch the front desk—and the door. This isn't your busy time of day anyway, is it?"

After climbing the stairs—there was no elevator—they stood in a dark hall in front of an even darker door.

"Unlock the door," Devorkian said in a low voice.

"But there's someone still in there."

Devorkian put his finger to his lips. His lips formed the words, "Unlock it."

Cocker turned the key, then allowed Devorkian to pull him back from the door. Devorkian knocked three times sharply.

There was no answer. Devorkian quietly turned the knob and pushed the door open. The room was dark and small and smelled worse than the lobby. The bed covers shifted, and a dark face with long, black, untidy hair appeared.

"Good morning," Detective Devorkian said.

"Good morning," said Sergeant Prestwyck. He held out his hand to a tall, thin, nervous-looking man in a gray suit. "I'm Sergeant Prestwyck."

The man's hands were sweaty, Prestwyck noticed when they shook hands.

"Thank you for coming," Prestwyck continued. "Did you bring the dental records?"

"Yes, they're right here. But . . ."

"Is something wrong, Dr. Spenser?"

"It's just that . . . they told us about it in dental school . . . but I've never had a request like this before. Grace Hutchinson was one of my patients."

"Yeah. This is not easy. It's pretty ugly, but it's murder, and we need to know who she is."

Spenser took a deep breath, nodded.

"Dr. Spenser, we will have the pathologist check the woman's teeth against the records you brought. But you knew Mrs. Hutchinson, and we have no one else to ask. This is unusual, but would you mind looking at the body?"

Spenser gulped. "Yes, I guess so. I do . . . have a . . . duty to my patients."

Spenser followed Prestwyck into the stainless steel room. After the drawer had been pulled out, Prestwyck paused before pulling off the sheet. "I want you to look at the woman and see if you recognize her—this will be hard because the front part of her face is gone. The public does not know this, and we would request that you not tell anyone about the condition of the face."

As Prestwyck slowly pulled back the sheet, Spenser gasped. The file, which he was still holding in his hand, slipped from his fingers, and pages scattered over the floor. He stood frozen and staring for what seemed a long time, perhaps a full minute.

"Well, Dr. Spenser? Is this Grace Hutchinson?"

Spenser took a deep breath, moved a step closer, and looked methodically over the woman's body. "I don't know," he said at last. "The part that I would remember . . . her face . . . it's . . . The hair is right. The body could be . . . well, I never saw her naked and . . ."

Spenser stooped suddenly and began picking up the papers and X-rays from the file. He turned from the body, placed the papers on a counter and carefully sorted them into their proper order. He turned back, but his resolve suddenly weakened, his knees buckled, and Dr. Spenser fell face forward onto the floor at Prestwyck's feet.

An hour later, Lazinski walked into Prestwyck's office.

"Well?" Prestwyck asked.

"Fifteen teeth left in the mouth. Four had fillings. Three of those were marked on Spenser's chart, but one of them wasn't on the right part of the tooth. The fourth filling isn't on the chart."

"What does that mean? This isn't Grace Hutchinson?"

"Several possibilities. The chart might be wrong. Spenser might have forgotten to put the fourth filling on the chart, or it might have been accidentally erased. Doubtful. She might have had another dentist do the fourth filling, but it doesn't look new. Therefore, in all probability, it's not Grace Hutchinson."

Prestwyck's shoulders sagged. "That's what the dentist thought. After he came to."

It was a surprisingly small rectangular room, divided lengthwise by a counter and a Plexiglas partition. Clint Granowski had never been here before. He sat down in a chair indicated to him. A steel door on the other side of the partition opened, and a tall man in blue jeans walked in. His hair stuck out at odd angles, and his eyes were bloodshot. He stared stupidly along the partition, his eyes bypassing Clint and then returning to focus on his face for a few seconds. He walked to the chair on the other side of the partition and sat down.

Clint spoke first. "Good morning, Gary. How—" He had been about to say, "How are you?" but realized it was a stupid question.

Gary Drummond cleared his throat and swallowed. "You, uh . . ." he began. "You said that sometime . . . we could talk . . . uh . . . Clint."

"Yeah, Gary. I'm glad you called me."

"They . . . they think I killed Grace!" the man suddenly blurted out.

It was a few moments before Clint could move. He forced himself to ask, "Did you?"

Drummond swallowed hard. "Wh-what?. . . Kill her? . . ."

"Have they charged you?"

"They're charging me this afternoon."

"With murder?"

Drummond shook his head violently. "Assault. I—I punched a cop . . . when they came to the house. I was so mad, I . . . at what I had done."

Clint swallowed. "What did you do, Gary? Did you kill her?"

"We had a big fight."

"You and the cop?"

"Grace . . . me and Grace. . . . I got drunk. . . . I pushed her against the wall."

"What did you fight about?"

"Kids. She couldn't have kids."

"Or . . . maybe you couldn't get her pregnant?"

Drummond rubbed his face with his hands. "God . . ."

Yes, Gary, God is exactly who you need. But Clint didn't say it out loud. Not yet. He leaned toward the Plexiglas and kept his voice gentle. "Gary, we know about your problem with not having children. Grace told Carol about it two months ago."

"Two months . . ."

"Gary, you will feel better if you tell me. Did you kill her?"

Drummond didn't seem to be listening. "They took me to the morgue . . . to see this body. She was just lying there, with her face all messed up . . . so white . . . so white . . ."

"Gary, was it Grace?"

"I looked and I looked . . . and I can't stop looking. I can't stop seeing. I saw . . . I recognized . . ."

"It was Grace?"

"I knew. . . . I recognized myself. . . . I saw myself. I knew that was where I was going."

"You realized you're going to die too? That's true. Not for this—we don't have the death penalty for murder in Canada. But yes, we are all going to die."

"Die . . . or . . . or kill . . ."

"Ah, I see. Guilt is more fearful than death. It really is a dreadful thing, when we really recognize our own sinfulness."

"She was dead. . . . It was awful. . . . I knew that was where I was headed. If I didn't stop . . . if I couldn't . . . it would be Grace lying there next."

"What are you saying, Gary? You killed another woman? It wasn't Grace you killed? Gary, do you have a lawyer?"

It was noon. The investigation team were packing up their equipment and loading it into vans—along with a black garbage bag full of Grace the prostitute's meager belongings. There wasn't much.

The team at the rear of the building had stopped and questioned five men who had tried to sneak out the back way. It wasn't legal perhaps, but they had arrested two of them—for old, unrelated offenses.

Devorkian had questioned Mary LeClair, the woman currently occupying the room. Her hair was black, but she wore it long, was too tall at five-foot-eight, and definitely did not wear white. She was nineteen, looked forty, and was a user. They found a small rock of crack and a bag of marijuana in her room. After the fingerprint team had finished with the room, she and Devorkian had gone over every article in the room piece by piece. The drugs were the only item she identified as not being hers—"Must've been left by that other girl. . . . Grace, did you say her name was?"

They hadn't charged her. Their only excuse for continuing

to use the search warrant after they learned the room had been rented again was that Grace might have left something behind. They couldn't use the search warrant under those circumstances and then insist that the drugs must belong to the new occupant of the room. Devorkian knew what a good lawyer would do with *that* in a courtroom.

"I got something." Osnachuck breezed into Prestwyck's office.

"What?"

"I got something. The phone calls. I finally reached one of the numbers in Grace Hutchinson's phone book."

"Who?"

"Woman named Alice McIntyre. She says she's Grace Hutchinson's aunt. Lives in Toronto. Says Grace's husband died of cancer a year ago. It was kind of tragic. He was only thirty-two, and they had moved to Winnipeg about a year before that. And Grace has no living parents, brothers, or sisters."

"What about Grace? Does she know where Grace is?"

"No. She says Grace left a message on her answering machine three or four weeks ago, saying she was going away on a trip—that it had come up suddenly and the aunt shouldn't worry if she didn't hear from her for a while."

"Did the message say where she was going?"

"No. Grace also didn't say how she was going to get there."

"Well, we know she didn't use her car. What about the voice? Did the aunt say it sounded like Grace?"

"I asked her about that. She said she didn't think anything of it at the time, of course."

"But?"

"But come to think of it, Grace's voice had sounded a bit different. The aunt had just figured maybe she was excited."

"How different? Higher? Lower? Was there unusual background noise?"

"The aunt wasn't sure—just different. And naturally she erased the message, so we can't have it analyzed. Shall I keep checking on Hutchinson?"

"Yeah. She probably isn't our body, but she definitely is missing. At least check the airlines and travel agents."

"I've already started on that, but nothing so far. The airlines say no one named Grace Hutchinson flew out of Winnipeg that weekend, but I'll keep checking."

Osnachuck turned to go, but paused in the doorway.

"What is it?" Prestwyck snapped.

"You don't believe that stuff in the paper, do you? About there maybe being three women murdered?"

"No way. Ledyear is an idiot. But we won't let that stop us from doing a thorough job, understand?"

Scott Ledyear's stubby finger found the listing in the phone book, then punched in the numbers. The phone rang eight times before Harry Collins's tired, jovial voice said, "Grace Mission."

Devorkian stood, stretched, and stared out the window. It was the end of what had turned out to be a frustrating day. He had pushed ahead with his investigations and there were still good possibilities, but somehow he was unsatisfied. Something didn't feel right. It felt as if he was barking up the wrong tree.

Constable Martin paused in the doorway, knocked quickly, and proceeded into the room. "Detective Devorkian . . ."

Devorkian whirled. "What?"

"We've been combing the streets, talking to the street people, the hookers and winos."

"Sounds like fun to me."

Martin hesitated. He didn't know Devorkian well enough to know if this was a joke or not. "Anyway," he continued, "we got something. Two hookers remember Grace getting into an older model white Cadillac. They knew Grace—they weren't friends or anything, but they had seen her around. They remembered the white Cadillac because they hadn't seen it around before. And the pickup was a bit strange. They said the guy had been cruising around for a while, but he didn't stop until he saw Grace. Grace approached the car, but the prostitutes wondered if she knew the guy because as soon as she got close, she stopped and started to back away. The guy got out of the car and grabbed her."

"What do you mean grabbed her? Kidnapped her?"

"No. Grabbed her by the arm and then talked to her. The hookers said Grace and the guy must have talked about ten minutes, but they weren't close enough to hear what they were saying. They said Grace seemed agitated at first, and angry, but she calmed down after a while and got in the car. They drove off, and the prostitutes say that was the last time they saw Grace."

"I don't suppose they remember when this happened."

"No. About a month, they thought."

"And, of course, they didn't get a license plate number."

"No, but they did notice it was an Ontario plate."

"Ontario, eh?"

"The body was found on the highway to Ontario, right?"

"Yes, but that doesn't get us very far. Do you have any idea how many white Cadillacs there are in Ontario?"

"I would guess there are lots."

"What did the prostitutes have to say about the man? Did you get a description?"

"Not as good as the car. It was dark."

"Of course."

"They said he was young, dark hair, in his twenties maybe. He was taller than Grace, maybe five-eight or five-ten. They described his clothes as dark."

"Dark?"

"Yeah, dark."

"Let me guess, these girls are users, right?"

Martin shrugged. "What do you expect? All those girls are."

"All but Grace." Devorkian smiled. "Thanks, Martin. That's good work. Keep at it."

Martin should keep at it, but Devorkian was tired. He was going home.

Chapter 17

WEDNESDAY, JULY 17

The newspaper landed with a thump on the desk. Jake Pendanz smiled warmly as he looked down. He was a tall, slightly paunchy man with prematurely white hair. "Have you seen this?" he asked.

John Smyth looked up and smiled back. "Who has time to read?" he asked. Editor humor.

The headline blared: "Serial killer?" The subheading asked: "Is unknown man stalking Graces?"

It was another front-page special by Scott Ledyear. Smyth picked up the newspaper and began reading methodically, an old proofreader's habit. Jake Pendanz dropped into the chair across from the desk.

"Could a serial killer be stalking Winnipeg women?" read Ledyear's lead sentence. He then used up some space summarizing some of what he had written yesterday; Smyth wondered whether Ledyear was being paid by the word. The gist of Ledyear's article was that there were now three missing women named Grace. "Some wonder," he suggested, "whether this is a coincidence. Could it be that a serial killer is out there, stalking and killing women named Grace?"

Not content to merely pose rhetorical questions, Ledyear had sought out an expert who could provide an authoritative answer—a psychiatrist named Myron Thuringer. Not only did Dr. Thuringer have a thriving practice, Ledyear reported; but also he had written several learned articles on abnormal psychology. John Smyth grimaced. Like many church people, he had an inherent distrust of psychiatrists. Pastors had a better track record at curing diseases of the soul than psychiatrists, he believed, although he was willing to admit that psychiatrists were sometimes better at describing them.

"I don't want to create a panic," Ledyear quoted Dr. Thuringer as saying, "and we don't know for sure that more than one woman has been killed, but the fact that three women named Grace are missing is suggestive. It is certainly possible that someone could be stalking women named Grace. It makes sense psychologically."

But why would someone go around killing women he didn't know just because they were named Grace? Scott Ledyear was sure his readers must be asking that question, so he asked it for them.

"It is not as strange as it might sound. The killer would not be rational, of course. There wouldn't be a *logical, practical* reason for committing the murders, but there might be a *psychological* reason."

Could the learned doctor suggest such a psychological reason?

As a matter of fact, he could. "One possibility does come to mind, but remember that it is only a theory. Grace is not just a woman's name. It is also a common word in Christian circles and is used a lot by the so-called evangelical or fundamentalist groups. There is even a Christian denomination called the Grace Church.

"Grace is supposed to be the goodness of God to people. Love, material wealth—everything good—is said to be a gift from God. But there is a paradox, especially for the more conservative Christians, who are supposedly given all these things by God but not allowed to enjoy them. The church makes them feel guilty if they have money. So to relieve them from their guilt, to 'save' them, so to speak, the church offers to take the money off their hands in the form of donations. Sex is another thing, and here's where the theory becomes relevant to these murders. Women are a gift from God, but sex is considered evil, so that creates tremendous psychological pressure. Men are given women but not allowed to make love to them. It can drive them crazy—quite literally. The repressed sexual tension builds up to the point that some individuals crack under the strain. If there is a serial killer, I would look for him in the evangelical church pews, or it could be someone who was raised under the influence of an evangelical church and has left it—because the scars still remain."

Smyth put down the newspaper. "Where do these guys get this nonsense?" he asked. "How can he talk about God's grace just in terms of sex and material things?"

"You know the answer," Jake Pendanz replied. "The man doesn't have a clue what grace really means."

John sighed. "But hasn't he even read the studies? Doesn't he know that evangelical Christians on average are happier and healthier, both mentally and physically, than other people? Doesn't he know that married evangelicals enjoy sex more than other people do, married or single?"

"Not just that," Jake Pendanz replied with a straight face. "Doesn't he know that in all the new evangelical churches nowadays, people sit on chairs rather than pews?"

The steel door to the interview room opened, and Gary Drummond shuffled through it. He paused, looked around the room, and froze. Slowly he approached the Plexiglas partition. He did not sit down.

"Hello, Gary," she said.

"It's . . . you." He had been told he had a visitor, and he had been expecting to see Clint Granowski. "When . . . how did you get here? Where have you been?"

"Osnachuck!"

"Yes, sir," Osnachuck hurried into Prestwyck's office. Prestwyck had been in for half an hour, and was angry that Osnachuck had not reported yet.

"What have you found out about Grace Hutchinson?"

"We've reached all the major travel agencies."

"And?"

"So far, none of them has any record of a Grace Hutchinson taking a trip or even making an inquiry in the past month or two."

"Have you checked them all?"

"All the major ones. There are some small ones that aren't open yet today. We're still working on them. She didn't have a computer, so chances are she didn't use an online service, but—"

"What about earlier?"

"Earlier?"

"Yes, earlier trips. Did she have a regular travel agent?"

"I—I don't know."

"You didn't check, did you?"

"No, I—"

"Do it."

"Yes, sir."

At that same moment, Constable Hansson burst into Devorkian's office. "You'd better come. There's a woman here to see Gary Drummond. She gave her name as Grace Drummond!"

Devorkian's jaw dropped. Then he sucked in his breath. "Let them talk. We'll see her when they're done. We haven't charged him with murder."

Another thought struck him. "And go pick up Louise Crocker."

"John," Jake Pendanz said. "Can I ask you a personal question?"

"Sure."

"How are you doing with all this?"

"What, the murder and everything?"

"Yes. Do you want to talk about it?"

"Well, the whole thing is pretty upsetting. I mean, I think I saw a human being kill another human being. And the police are a problem—the way they act. It's like they really think I did something—that I'm lying or I killed the woman myself."

"From the airplane?"

"I don't know. Actually, I think they're just trying to shake up everybody, make everybody involved nervous until somebody makes a mistake."

"John, I am sorry to have to ask this, but *are* you nervous? Will you . . . make a mistake?"

"Jake, I make lots of mistakes, but no, I'm not guilty of anything that would interest the police. And yeah, I *am* a little nervous. Just human nature, I guess—you're under suspicion, so you feel guilty, even if you've done nothing wrong. But of course everybody has done *something* wrong."

Jake nodded. "Thanks for answering. And I know what you mean. You ask for forgiveness and you know you're forgiven. But you don't really forget, even if God does."

"Which is one reason we need so much grace," Smyth said. "Anyway, thanks for asking about it—and Ruby and I appreciate your prayers. But don't worry. It bothers me, but I'm doing okay. I'm handling it."

"No, it's okay, Mary Alice. I mean I'm handling it okay. But what if I'm wrong about Grace? It's not like I can be sure. And I'm not talking to that nosy reporter Scott Ledyear anymore."

"Now, Louise, I know Scott Ledyear is a jerk, but we have to learn how to make use of men like that. We need to use the media for our cause. They can be very useful to us if we use them right."

"I know, Mary Alice, it's just that . . . I mean . . ."

"Louise, there's not a mean bone in your body."

"Oh, I'm going to have to hang up now. There's someone at the door. I hope it isn't the police again."

"Thank you for agreeing to talk to us, Mrs. Drummond."

They were sitting in a small interview room, and Devorkian was at his most charming. "Please understand. You were reported missing by your husband, so we have been looking for you for some time. We have to be careful about these things—sometimes it may seem ridiculously so. Would it be possible for you to show us some identification?"

Mrs. Drummond began fumbling in her purse and finally produced a small wallet. She handed it to Devorkian, who flipped through the plastic pages. The photo driver's license was either authentic or a good fake.

"Would you mind telling us where you have been for the past month?"

"I have a friend who has a ranch out in Alberta. I needed time to think, and I asked her not to tell anyone I was there. I just stayed there and helped with the chores. She's a good friend. She let me stay without pushing me to make up my mind."

"And did you make up your mind?"

"Yes. I decided to come back."

"To your husband?"

"Yes."

"But you told your husband that you were going to another man, a Johnny Cockerill."

"I was angry. That just popped into my head."

"Who's Johnny Cockerill?"

"Just a boy I knew in high school. We never even dated. He was one of the hottest boys in school, and I was . . . It was silly. I was just trying to hit back at Gary."

"I see," Devorkian said. "When did you leave?"

"On June sixteenth, early in the morning. It was a Sunday."

"Why did you leave?"

"We had had a big argument the night before."

"An argument or a fight, Mrs. Drummond?"

"An argument."

"Did your husband hit you, Mrs. Drummond?"

"Not then. He pushed me a couple of times against the wall."

"But he'd hit you before?"

"Just once, about six months ago."

Devorkian looked at Hosschuk. Either Gary Drummond was telling the truth, or they had agreed on the details of their story. He wished he could have interviewed Mrs. Drummond before she had a chance to talk to her husband, but by the time he learned she was talking to Drummond, it had been too late. He continued, "Are you aware that that is a criminal act?"

"What? Gary hitting me?"

"Yes. You could charge him with assault."

"But I have no intention of charging my husband."

"He will do it again."

"I don't think so. He's changed."

There was a sudden clunk and some scurrying feet outside the room. Devorkian excused himself and stepped out the door.

In the room next door, Louise Crocker was lying on the floor, Hosschuk and another policeman bent over her. Hosschuk was patting her hand. He looked up. "She fainted," he said.

"Did she see Mrs. Drummond through the window?"

"Yes."

"What did she say?"

"Nothing. That's when she fainted."

"I'm going back to Mrs. Drummond. Call me when Mrs. Crocker is able to talk."

It was a full fifteen minutes before Devorkian was summoned to interview Louise Crocker. During that time, he had continued to ask Grace Drummond questions, but had discovered little more. She admitted readily that Gary had had a handgun, but Devorkian couldn't ask her to identify it because it was still in the forensics lab. She confirmed her husband had bought the gun when he was working extra shifts as a night watchman at work. She didn't know if he had a permit and didn't seem to know that he needed one. In all areas, her story was consistent, and Devorkian had been unable to frame a question that would trip her up.

"Hello, Mrs. Crocker," Devorkian said. "Are you feeling better?"

"Yes. I guess I just fainted. It was the shock. I'm sorry."

"There's nothing to be sorry about, Mrs. Crocker."

"Oh, but there is! That poor woman. I mean, I told you

that woman in the morgue was dead, and now she's alive."

"The woman in the morgue *is* dead, Mrs. Crocker."

"Yes, but I mean she wasn't Grace Drummond, was she? And I said she was."

"Are you saying the woman in the next room is Grace Drummond?"

"Yes. Oh, yes."

"Are you sure?"

"Yes, I'm sure. Oh, but I told you that last time too, didn't I?"

"No, Mrs. Crocker. You said you *thought* it was Grace Drummond. The body *was* hard to identify."

"But I misled you, and I told everybody . . . Oh, I'm so embarrassed."

Devorkian squared his shoulders and took up his sternest policeman's voice. "Mrs. Crocker, that is enough of that!" he said. "We do not blame you for anything. You did your duty as a citizen. We asked for help, and you stepped forward with information. You are to be commended, Mrs. Crocker. I wish more citizens were as conscientious as you."

"Oh," she said. "I guess I was, wasn't I?"

"Thank you for coming in again. A policeman will drive you home shortly. Good-bye, Mrs. Crocker."

Devorkian motioned with his head, and Hosschuk followed him out into the corridor and shut the door.

"What do you think?" Devorkian asked.

"Oh, it's Grace Drummond all right, unless Mrs. Crocker is in on it too. After she came around, she had another look. I'm sure she recognized her. And the faint was real enough. She was shocked."

"You hadn't told her ahead of time who you wanted her to identify?"

"No."

"Do you think she might have guessed?"

"Maybe, but she's not a rocket scientist."

"True."

"So what are we going to do with Gary Drummond?"

"Mrs. Drummond has apparently talked to a man named Clint Granowski, and he is arranging bail."

"Granowski's the guy who came to see him yesterday. Do you think Granowski and Drummond might be in on something together?"

"Didn't you check him out?"

"Not yet. I haven't had time."

"She says he's their minister."

"Sounds suspicious to me. I didn't think Drummond was the kind of guy who's into religion."

"Maybe he got religion after being here. Evidently the Drummonds don't go to church, but they have been talking to this guy Granowski."

"What church does he belong to?"

"I don't know. Mrs. Drummond couldn't remember the name. You'll find out when you check out Granowski."

"Oh. That's an order, right?"

"It's a joy to work with Rhodes scholars."

"All right . . . uh, sir? What are you going to do with Drummond's charges?"

"The assault charge is still valid, but I don't want to go into court and have to explain why we arrested him in the first place. And we've got the gun with no permit, so we can use that if we have to. I don't think there's much chance he will sue us for false arrest. We'll keep the gun, let things sit for a couple of weeks, and then quietly drop the charges."

"But it doesn't really help us with our problem, does it?"

"What's that?"

"Who Grace is."

"No, it does not . . . but it's really an RCMP case, anyway."

The desk and office were as cluttered as ever. John Smyth sat amid the chaos, trying to concentrate on editing reports and having a hard time with it. The article by Scott Ledyear had disturbed him. The clamor of the telephone disturbed him even more, and he jumped involuntarily.

"John Smyth," he said.

"Mr. Smyth, this is Scott Ledyear of the *Winnipeg New Times*. Perhaps you have read some of my articles."

Speak of the devil, Smyth thought, then shuddered. After today's article, the expression seemed too apt. "Yes, I have read some of your articles."

"Yes, good. I understand you're a journalist too. We should maybe get together sometime and talk shop." This was flattery. Smyth felt sure Ledyear did not actually consider an editor of a church magazine to be a brother journalist. He no doubt assumed Smyth wasn't very intelligent and wouldn't catch on.

"Okay." Smyth was noncommittal. "What can I do for you today?"

"I'm working on a story about the murdered woman who was found two or three weeks ago, the woman named Grace."

"Yes."

"I was talking to Harry Collins yesterday, and he told me you may have seen the murder."

Smyth said nothing. He had been expecting something like this and wondering what he would say.

"Mr. Smyth, can you confirm that you saw the murder?"

"No. I mean the police asked me not to comment on that."

"So you did see the murder?"

"I saw something, but I'm really not supposed to talk about it."

"And is it true that you saw this from an airplane?"

"I was on an airplane, but I can't tell you—"

"What were you doing on the airplane?"

"What does anyone do on an airplane? I was flying home—from a conference in Alberta."

"And what exactly did you see?"

"I really can't talk about that."

"You are a member of the Grace Church?"

"Yes."

"And editor of *Grace* magazine?"

"Yes."

"What did you see, Mr. Smyth? Was it a member of Grace Church?"

"What!?"

"Who did you see? Was it a member of Grace Church?"

"No! I don't know. I really can't say."

"That means it was."

"No."

"Come on, Mr. Smyth, you are an editor. You believe in the free flow of information. The public has a right to know. What should I tell them?"

"You can tell them I have no comment."

Smyth put the receiver down with force. The problem was that he *did* believe in the free flow of information, in openness. How many times had he been on the other end of such a phone call? How many times had he pleaded with a pastor or church leader to give him some information so that he could print the truth? He had used all the arguments. The truth is seldom as bad as the rumors that will fly if the facts are kept hidden. It is only as problems are discussed openly that they can be solved. But there was that police order that he keep silent. . . .

That was a rationalization, Smyth realized. The truth was he did not want to talk to Scott Ledyear. He did not want to tell him he thought he had seen a murder from an airplane.

He knew how he would sound if Ledyear printed that—like a fundamentalist fanatic guided by delusions of his own importance or a weak-minded fool prone to hallucination. He was afraid of what Ledyear would write, of how it would make him sound. And what was Ledyear really looking for? Was he trying to find an evangelical Christian he could blame the murder on, a Grace Church Christian? What would tomorrow's headline read? Would Smyth himself, or one of his colleagues, be suspected of murder?

In that moment, John Smyth became aware that he was afraid of the press. He was suddenly afraid of the power that the press wields, that he himself wielded. How many times had he told a reluctant witness, "You can trust me to write it fairly." But they hadn't always agreed to trust him, and then he had railed against those who had something to hide and were foolishly thinking they could cover up the truth. It would all come out anyhow. But would it come out? And what if the writer made a mistake in how he presented the facts? It was so easy to destroy someone's life with the written word.

But isn't there a difference? he wondered. Scott Ledyear would write anything as long as it was sensational, just to sell newspapers. Smyth, however, had a disinterested passion for truth and a compassion for the people involved. The regular press have no Christian concern, he reasoned. They want to *know* more than they want to help.

"But I want to know too!" he mumbled emphatically. "I want to know too."

It wasn't going to be pleasant, but it had to be done. Mike Hosschuk squared his shoulders and stepped into Devorkian's office. "I have the lab reports," he said.

"From what? Drummond's house or the hotel?"

"From both."

"And?"

"We could find no fingerprints in Drummond's house matching the fingerprints of the dead woman."

"Now there's a news flash, considering we both saw Grace Drummond alive this morning. What about the gun?"

"Just because the dead woman isn't Grace Drummond doesn't mean Drummond couldn't still have done it."

"Right, he murdered some other guy's wife."

Hosschuk shrugged.

"What about the gun?"

"Ballistics says that Drummond's gun did not fire the shot that killed the dead woman."

"So he borrowed the other guy's gun too? Get on with it. You know we're looking at the other Grace, the prostitute, now."

"No, we're not. No fingerprints in the hotel room matched the dead woman's either."

"What! None?"

"Nope."

"Is Bill Cocker lying to us? Did he send us to the wrong room?"

"I don't know."

"Well, check. Talk to the other residents. Talk to some johns. Or maybe the prints have been wiped off."

"I don't think so. The place looked like it hadn't been cleaned in months. There were lots of old prints—that's the good news."

"Old prints?"

"Yeah. I bet half the bad guys in western Canada passed through that room at one time or another. The computer made four positive identifications—not counting the current tenant, of course—and six possibles, including one Randolph Williams."

"Who? Wait . . . not *the* Randolph Williams?"

"That's him. Wanted in three U.S. states as a serial murderer and rapist."

"Wow. Get on that one."

"Trouble is, like I said, it's an old print. We only found one, and it was on the underside of the bed frame."

Devorkian sighed. "It doesn't get any easier, does it?"

"Nope. Shall I tell the FBI anyway?"

"Sure. Maybe they can do something with it. Maybe they can figure out a way to date fingerprints."

The phone rang and Devorkian picked up. It was Sergeant Prestwyck. "Thanks for phoning back. I thought maybe you would want to call another press conference."

"Why?" Prestwyck sounded suspicious.

"Because we have released Gary Drummond."

"What am I supposed to tell the press—that the Winnipeg police are incompetent? Why did you let him go?"

"Because an unexpected visitor came to see him this morning. His wife."

Prestwyck swore. "Was she alive?"

"Looked like it to me."

"So she's not our body either. Tell you what. Write up a news release, sign it, and fax it to me. I'll sign it too and then fax it to the media."

"What? No press conference?"

"Not in this lifetime!" Prestwyck slammed down the receiver, but Devorkian, experienced, had already pulled the handset away from his ear.

"That was Prestwyck," Devorkian told his sergeant. "He wants to issue a news release. Doesn't want to hold a press conference."

"Do you?"

"No way. If I ever see Scott Ledyear or Mary Alice Bruckner again this side of hell, it will be too soon."

The phone rang again.

"Devorkian."

"Detective Devorkian, this is Scott Ledyear of the *Winnipeg New Times.*"

Speak of the devil, thought Devorkian rather unoriginally. "Ah, Mr. Ledyear," he said into the phone. "I was just preparing a news release for you. You might be interested to know that the police have found Grace Drummond. She is not missing after all. She is not the murdered woman. Perhaps you would be interested in writing a retraction—"

"I've got a more important question right now. Did a man named John Smyth witness the murder of the woman named Grace from an airplane?" Ledyear was obviously hurrying to get the question in before Devorkian hung up.

"Did he tell you that?"

"He confirmed it." The slight hesitation in Ledyear's voice told Devorkian that Smyth had done nothing of the sort.

"There's nothing to that story, Mr. Ledyear. Mr. Smyth, like many other people, offered some information, which the police followed up. It was checked out thoroughly, and there is no evidence that Mr. Smyth saw anything at all or that anything he might have seen is even remotely connected to the case of the murdered woman."

"So he did see something?"

"We don't know that."

"Is it true, then, that the police knew about the murder two weeks before the body was found and did nothing?"

"We didn't do nothing. We checked out—look, why don't you address these questions to Sergeant Prestwyck of the RCMP? He's the one who talked to Mr. Smyth."

"I did," Ledyear admitted. "He hung up on me."

"Wise man." And Devorkian did likewise.

Chapter 18

THURSDAY, JULY 18

It had become a required morning ritual for all of them—reading the morning paper for the latest installment in Scott Ledyear's epic. They were addicted, compelled to read as fans are compelled to watch the next episode of a soap opera. They might be horrified at what they saw, but they had to know or they couldn't go on with their day.

John Smyth had picked up a copy of today's *Winnipeg New Times* at the corner store on his way to work, but did not open it until he had gone into his office, shut the door, and sat down behind his cluttered desk.

"Did police fumble delay investigation?" blared the headline. The article stated, "The *New Times* has learned that an eyewitness may have reported the murder of the unknown woman named Grace on the day she was murdered—two weeks before Grace's body was found in a woods east of Winnipeg.

"Another startling fact is that the witness provides a link

to the fundamentalist Grace Church, which psychiatrist Myron Thuringer, in an exclusive story in yesterday's *New Times,* said might be connected to the murder."

The story went on to say that one John Smith, a member of the hierarchy of Grace Church, had apparently told police he had seen the murder of a woman through the window of an airplane just before it landed at Winnipeg Airport. "The police would not confirm this, and Mr. Smith refused to talk to a reporter."

There was more to the article, including comments on the latest developments from Myron Thuringer, but John Smyth had had enough for now. He dropped the paper on his cluttered desk and leaned back in his worn chair. "He didn't even spell my name right," he muttered.

The newspaper also lay face up on Devorkian's desk.

"Full of good news, is it, sir?"

"Funny, Hosschuk. After all that stuff he printed about the Drummonds and the women finding out who Grace was and who the killer was, we prove it is all nonsense, and what does he do with the information? Buried it in a one-inch box next to a front-page article full of more innuendo."

"I guess he prefers to bury his mistakes."

"I'd like to bury him."

"Or convict him of murder."

"That would be a pleasure, all right. He doesn't even have the guts to admit he was wrong. All it says is that Grace Drummond has turned up, implying that the police were idiots for thinking she was missing in the first place."

"Maybe it would have gotten more attention if you'd held a press conference instead of just sending a fax."

Devorkian scowled. "Typical of Ledyear," he said. "The facts get an inch, and speculation gets the lead story."

"I'm not sure it's all speculation, sir."

"What?"

"I checked out that Granowski guy, the one who visited Drummond and then bailed him out after his wife got home. He really is a pastor."

"So?"

"Care to guess the denomination?"

"You're kidding."

"Nope. Pastor of New Life Community Church. It's affiliated with Grace Evangelical Church of North America."

Devorkian was thoughtful. "So where does that lead us? Do you think Granowski could be the guy?"

"Maybe it leads us back to Drummond."

"Yes, but then who did he kill—and why? Because his wife left him and the dead woman reminded him of his wife? Because of that religious repression mumbo-jumbo of Dr. What's-his-name, the psychiatrist? And how do we link him to the other Graces? . . . Wait a minute. What kind of car does he have?"

"I don't remember. It was black."

"It was black all right. But what make was it?"

It was very early for David Mackenzie—nine-thirty in the morning—but nothing had been the same lately. He had not been keeping his regular hours. He was having trouble sleeping. He shivered in the early morning breeze that scurried papers along the sidewalk in front of him. They reminded him of leaves, but white and gray leaves, unnatural, as if they were diseased or he was in a dream. It seemed to him that he had been in a dream for a long time, sleepwalking, not really awake to the life that was going on around him.

His steps carried him along the by-now-familiar route up Main Street. He paused at the grimy storefront. He did not usually come here this early in the morning, but no one else would be around.

He tried the door handle. It was locked. Then he did something unusual. He knocked. He, David Mackenzie, knocked on a door, asking to be admitted to a place where he had not been invited. He knocked, and when no one came he knocked again, louder. When still no one came, he began kicking at the door with his foot.

Suddenly the door gave way, and he fell forward into the dark interior. Slowly he rolled over and moved into a sitting position. He looked up into the round face of Harry Collins.

Harry smiled, then sat down on the floor in front of David. "Good morning," he said.

"Morning," David mumbled after a while.

Harry just sat and smiled, waiting, as if he knew there was more. And at last the words came. David's jaw worked, his head bobbed, and finally the words blurted out, "Where is she? Where has she gone?"

Strangely, that felt like a beginning.

Sergeant Prestwyck drummed his fingers on the desk, counting the rings of the telephone.

"Smyth," he almost shouted into the mouthpiece when the man finally answered. "This is Sergeant Prestwyck. I thought I told you not to talk to the press."

"I didn't. Harry Collins did."

"Who?"

"Harry Collins. He runs Grace Mission downtown. I gather he told Scott Ledyear what I saw—I mean might have saw—seen."

"I know Harry Collins. I've talked to him, remember. But listen—don't talk to anyone else. Do you understand?"

John Smyth's meek "Yes, sir" was drowned by the slamming of the receiver.

Constable Bisset entered the room. She hesitated momentarily at the sight of Prestwyck's angry face, then spoke: "There's someone to see you, sir."

"Who is it?"

"I don't know, sir. She wouldn't give her name. She insisted she talk to you personally."

Prestwyck sighed. Sometimes it seemed as if the criminals roamed free and got all the respect while the guardians of the public order were imprisoned in their own impotence. Dependent on information, they were at the beck and call of every person who claimed to know something and demanded to see them. "Show her in," he said.

A moment later a neat, well-dressed woman walked into the office. Her face was tanned, and she wore her dark hair cut short. Prestwyck guessed her age might be about thirty, but he wasn't sure. She was one of those trim women who would look thirty well into her fifties.

He stood and extended his hand. "Good morning," he said. "I am Sergeant Prestwyck. How can I help you?"

"Good morning," she replied. "I am Grace Hutchinson."

She sat down in the chair opposite the desk. For a moment Prestwyck remained standing with his hand out. He caught himself, eased down into the chair, and smiled.

"I understand you have been looking for me."

"Yes. Your apartment manager, Mrs. Plumtre, reported you missing. Your apartment was empty, but it didn't seem you had told anyone where you were going."

"I don't have any close relatives, Sergeant, and few friends here. I told my aunt in Toronto that I was going."

"Yes, but you didn't say *where* you were going."

"So you have been checking. No, she wasn't home, so I just left a message saying not to worry."

"But she wouldn't know how to reach you if it became necessary."

"No. That would have been difficult."

"Where were you?"

"This is a bit awkward; I guess a bit of a confession. A friend of mine, Megan Withers, and a friend of hers were planning on a Caribbean cruise. They found this fabulous deal, and so it wasn't really that expensive, considering. But then at the last moment Megan's friend had an accident; she broke her leg and couldn't go. So she and Megan asked if I would like to go in her place. They didn't want to just cancel because you have to pay in advance, but the reservations were all in her name. You're supposed to tell the cruise company and let them resell the tickets. That was one of the conditions that kept the price so low—I guess they get a fair number of cancellations and they get to sell some of the tickets twice. Also, there was no time to get a passport or vaccinations. So for the last three weeks I have been on a cruise ship masquerading as Pam Stuart. I took quite a risk, but it seemed like such a great opportunity. Pam and I look quite a bit alike, and no one looked at her passport photo very closely, so it worked. It was good to get away, but I'm afraid I may be guilty of something illegal."

Prestwyck smiled. "A Caribbean cruise? It's not likely to be my jurisdiction. I presume you can prove all this?"

The woman reached into her purse and pulled out a driver's license, some credit cards, and a bulging white envelope. "These are my receipts for the trip. I can give you the address of both Megan Withers and Pam Stuart, but maybe I should talk to them first so they will know it's okay to tell you the truth. Our photos won't be back for a few days."

"How did you know we were looking for you?"

"I got back late yesterday, and then this morning I ran into Mrs. Plumtre, and she just about fell over with shock. I asked her what was wrong, and she said she had reported me missing and you had searched my apartment. She found the card you had left her, so I just came down here immediately."

"I'm sorry we had to search your apartment, Mrs. Hutchinson. But, as you may know, we found a woman's body that fit your description. You were missing, so we had to check it out."

"That's all right, Sergeant. In a way . . . well, it was nice that someone noticed I was gone. I didn't expect to be missed."

"May I ask you a couple more questions, Mrs. Hutchinson? Why didn't you pay the rent before you left?"

"I actually got a check ready for Mrs. Plumtre, but things were so rushed I forgot to give it to her. I left it sitting on the side table by the front door."

"Yes, that's where we found it. May I ask one more question?"

"Certainly, Sergeant."

"There were no pictures of you—in fact, hardly any pictures at all—in your apartment."

"My husband died a year ago, Sergeant, and, well, it was very painful. So one night I just packed up all my pictures and took them over to Megan's house and asked her to keep them awhile. It was just too painful to look at them. But I think I may be getting ready to ask for them back. This trip was just what I needed."

John Smyth had considered not going to the meeting of the First and Third Thursday Winnipeg Grace Pastors and Wives Prayer Fellowship. But Ruby had taken charge. "We're going," she'd said. "It will help take your mind off the other thing." She had called a baby-sitter, and they had gone together.

The meeting this evening was in the basement of Central Grace Church, an old, rambling, brick structure just a few blocks from the Smyth house. They parked their station wagon in front of the church and walked around to the side to a heavy wooden door. Once inside, they turned to the right and descended the creaking staircase to a small, windowless hall. About thirty metal-and-wood stacking chairs had been set out in a circle, and twenty people—mostly men, with a few women—stood around a metal coffeemaker at one side.

The round figure of Harry Collins detached itself from the cluster and walked purposefully toward them. "John, Ruby," he said. "It's good to see you."

"Hi, Harry," Ruby responded. John nodded warily.

Gripping John's arm, Harry continued, "John, I wanted to tell you right away. I got a phone call from Lilly Greiss today, late this afternoon."

"Who?"

"Lilly Greiss—that's her real name, but you wouldn't know that. I'm talking about Grace—you know, the prostitute who was missing. She phoned me from Ontario. Dryden. She said her real name is Lilly White Greiss, but she went by Grace White here in Winnipeg."

"Who could blame her?" Ruby put in. "Lilly White! What an awful name! What kind of parents would do that to a child?"

"Well, I guess it was a family name or something. Her family life wasn't that happy anyway. Her parents are divorced, and her mother married a man named Greiss when Lilly was about thirteen. He evidently began abusing her sexually a year or so ago, until finally she ran away. I didn't get all the details—I'm going to be talking to her again. But for some reason, a couple of months ago, the stepfather got to feeling guilty and—this is the exciting part—he went to the police and turned himself in. I haven't found out why yet, but the couple evidently had started going to church. That was all Grace knew. Anyway, when he confessed, her brother Tom got in his Cadillac and drove out here looking for her. I think she had phoned him once, so he had some idea where to look."

"Harry, are you sure it was the same woman, not someone else pretending to be her?"

"What a strange question. Why would anyone want to impersonate her? But yes, I think it was her. It sounded like her. I'd never talked to her on the phone before, and she sounded a bit different, but then she would—she was home and off the street."

"Did you phone the police and tell them this?" John asked.

"Yes," Ruby put in, "instead of getting John to do your dirty work?"

"I did. I talked to a man at the city police named Martin—he works the downtown area—and I gave him Grace's phone number. He was just going off shift, but he said he would pass the message on and would come to see me tomorrow morning. I was just as glad about that, because I wanted to come here tonight."

"It's time to get started," Clint Granowski announced. The cluster of people slowly drifted away from the coffeemaker, and everyone sat down in the circle of chairs.

They sang a song or two—not very well, but the music helped set the tone for the evening. Clint, whose turn it was to lead, said a short prayer and then read a passage from 2 Samuel. It concerned King David, who had been a very virtuous and godly ruler of Israel but who had then inexplicably gone wrong—carrying on an affair with another man's wife and then having the husband murdered so he wouldn't find out. Clint pointed out the terrible cost of David's sin, how it had led to sexual sins and murder by his own sons as well as disaster for the kingdom. He then urged the pastors to take care that they did not fail as David had done.

The "sharing" then began. Several pastors and wives requested prayer for various needs or for people they were working with. John Smyth had trouble concentrating during this time. Should he ask for prayer? And for what? How would he phrase his request?

"Clint and I have a couple of items," Carol was saying. "We would like continued prayer for our next-door neighbors, Randy Campani and his wife, Moira. Randy is still very hard to get to know—not exactly rude, but he doesn't seem to want to talk at all. But that's the bad news. Clint, why don't you tell the good news?"

"Yes. This is really exciting. You know about Gary and Grace Drummond. You probably read about them in the papers. They weren't getting along, and Grace left Gary about a month ago. In fact, the police arrested Gary because they thought he might have murdered her. Well, she came back yesterday. I had already been to see him in jail. Anyway, because of all this, they both have been doing a lot of thinking."

"Haven't we all?" John Smyth whispered to Ruby.

"We had been trying to talk to them about Jesus and about their lives, but they wouldn't really open up. Well, now they're willing to talk. Carol and I spent most of the afternoon over at their place. They're not Christians yet, but they have agreed to counseling and they said they're going to come to church. I really believe they are very close."

Applause greeted Clint's words, but John Smyth did not applaud. His mind was elsewhere. The rest of the meeting was a blur. Pastors and wives voiced more requests for prayer, and the group spent a half-hour praying for the various items, but Smyth hardly heard any of it.

Sometimes answers to prayer are a long time coming. Sometimes they come more readily, and he was receiving such an answer now. He wasn't sure if the bells of heaven were ringing, though he rather thought they were, but bells were certainly ringing in his head—big bells, alarm bells, bells of recognition.

As soon as the last prayer was over, John leaned over and whispered to Ruby, "Excuse me. I want to talk to Clint a minute."

But Clint was busy, so he settled for saying a few words to Carol. Then he took Ruby by the hand and said, "Come on. I'm going to take you home. Then I'm going to the office for a few minutes. There's something I have to do."

"Go to the office?"

"I've changed my mind," Prestwyck said. "I've decided to let you have the case after all. I'm sure the murder took place in your jurisdiction."

"Thanks," Devorkian replied, "but no thanks."

It was nine o'clock in the evening, and Devorkian was sitting in Prestwyck's office, a box of day-old doughnuts and a backlog of frustration between them. They had talked earlier by telephone, and it had been Devorkian's idea to meet together to discuss possibilities. It was he who had brought the doughnuts.

"This isn't getting us anywhere," Devorkian continued. "Where are we really in this investigation? What do we really know?"

"Simple. We had three possibilities for the identity of the dead woman, and now we have none."

"Right, the three Graces, and all three have now turned up alive. They *have* turned up alive, haven't they?"

"Oh, yeah. Grace Hutchinson walked into my office this morning, and everything we've looked at says she's the real thing. How about your two? Any chance that one of them could be a phony?"

"I doubt it. Grace Drummond checks out, and I've spoken to Lilly Greiss on the phone. She lived over near Dryden—that's OPP jurisdiction. We'll have the local detachment confirm everything in the morning."

He let out a laugh. "All this wrangling over territory, and we end up waiting on the Ontario Provincial Police."

Prestwyck wasn't amused. "So much for victims. How about suspects?"

"All the suspects are directly connected to the supposed victims. Unless you fancy Gary Drummond picking up someone else's wife in someone else's car and killing her with someone else's gun."

Prestwyck grimaced. "You checked out Drummond's Cadillac?"

"Yes. It was originally black, and there's no evidence it was ever painted white and then painted black again."

"Then there's the psychiatrist's fancies."

"Yeah. Anyone who has ever been in contact with Grace Church, or maybe any other church. That really narrows it down."

There was a long pause as both men pondered the realities and the possibilities.

Finally, Devorkian broke the silence. "So where does that leave us?"

"Right back where we started from. With one dead body, identity unknown, no leads, and no suspects."

"And one religious writer who claims to have seen the murder from an airplane."

Ruby had been so surprised at John's unusual suggestion that he go back to the office so late in the evening that she had hardly protested. That would come later, John knew. He had left her with the hopeful words, "I won't be long."

Once at the office, he spent a few moments rummaging through the jumbled files, papers, and envelopes on his desk, and then he made two phone calls. The second was to RCMP headquarters.

"Prestwyck," the sergeant growled into the handset.

"Sergeant Prestwyck, this is John Smyth."

"The religious writer?"

"Yes."

"Speak of the . . ."

"I beg your pardon?"

"Never mind. What can I do for you, Mr. Smyth?"

"It's what I can do for you. I think I know who the dead woman is. Can I come to see you?"

"Now?"

"Yes. I'd rather get it over with."

"Sure. I'll be waiting."

After he had hung up, Prestwyck said to Devorkian, "It's John Smyth, the religious writer. He's coming to tell us who the murdered woman is."

"That's all we need. He's had another vision?"

Prestwyck shrugged and absentmindedly reached for a chocolate glazed.

Twenty minutes later, John Smyth walked into Sergeant Prestwyck's office.

"So you know who Grace is?" Devorkian asked after the pleasantries were over.

"I think I know who the dead woman is," Smyth replied. Reaching into a brown envelope, he pulled out two photographs. He handed the first to Prestwyck. "Is that the piece of jewelry the murdered woman had?"

The stiffening in Sergeant Prestwyck's face and body was almost imperceptible, but John Smyth, watching carefully, saw it. Prestwyck passed the photo without comment to Devorkian.

Smyth handed the second photo to Prestwyck. "Is that the murdered woman?" he asked.

Prestwyck examined the photo and passed it to Devorkian. "It could be," he said after a few moments. "Who is she?"

"I also think I know who killed her. I think I can take you to him—and to the place where she was murdered. However, I suggest we go there in my car, so as not to arouse suspicion."

Prestwyck and Devorkian sat motionless and speechless. Then Prestwyck looked at Devorkian. Devorkian shrugged.

"Okay with me," he said. "What have we got to lose?"

"I thought you said you had a car," Devorkian complained as Smyth's battered station wagon bumped through the streets of Winnipeg. It was often said of the city's streets: "Winnipeg has only two seasons—winter and construction."

Other than the occasional muttered comment, the three men rode in silence, each absorbed in his own thoughts. The car weaved its way toward the southwest section of Winnipeg, near the airport. It turned down Mapleleaf, a final quiet street, and pulled up in front of number 127, a white stucco house with a dull, reddish-brown roof. No word was said, but all three men got out of the car. The porch light of the white stucco house was on. Smyth led the way up the short sidewalk and rang the doorbell. Immediately a loud barking issued from inside the house.

In a moment, the door was opened by Carol Granowski. "John. Come in."

The dog, a tricolor Sheltie, ran up to them, turned and skittered down the hall, turned and came back, barking incessantly.

"Barney! No bark! Go lie down!" Clint Granowksi ordered from the doorway to the living room. The dog slithered into the living room and lay down under an end table, making only an occasional sound that was part bark, part growl, and part muttered complaint.

Smyth said, "This is Sergeant Prestwyck of the RCMP and Detective Devorkian of the Winnipeg Police. This is Clint and Carol Granowski—they are the pastor couple of a new church in this area."

"Granowski," Devorkian said. "You came to see Gary Drummond at the police station."

Clint seemed startled to have been recognized.

Carol said, "Let's go sit down in the living room. John, you said you were coming, so I made some coffee—and there's some fresh muffins." Carol was ever the gracious hostess. It was one of her great strengths as a pastor's wife. She loved doing things for people.

When they had sat down and received their coffee, Clint turned to the policemen sitting stiffly side by side on the sofa and asked, "I gather you wanted to talk to us about something."

John Smyth cleared his throat. "Actually, it was my idea to bring them here. I would like you to tell them about your next-door neighbors."

"Who? Randy and Moira?"

"Yes, particularly Moira."

"I never met her," Clint said suddenly.

"I was asking Carol," Smyth said.

"There's not much to tell. I met her only once. I was just going out. I was in the backyard on my way to the garage when Moira stuck her head over the fence. It's a pretty high fence, but I think she was standing on a stump—there's one near the fence on her side. Anyway, she said hello. It startled me because I hadn't noticed her, but she seemed very friendly. I was late for a meeting, but I was anxious to get to know the new neighbors, so I stopped and we talked for a few minutes. She asked if I knew where her husband was. I said I was sorry but we had not gotten to know Randy well yet and I hadn't seen him that day. I guess she had just arrived; he had moved here a week or two earlier. She wasn't supposed to be here for a couple more days, but she had come early and so he wasn't expecting her. She said she wanted to talk to him about something important. She seemed quite nervous about that. She wasn't sure how he would take it. She didn't say what it was. But she seemed so friendly and happy that I just flat out asked her if she was a Christian. She was really surprised. She said yes, she was, she had just become a Christian a couple of weeks before. It was in one of the Grace churches too, I think, but I didn't have time to ask her which one, because she interrupted me. She asked if I was a Christian, and when I said yes, she was very excited. She was hoping to find Christians here in Winnipeg and was amazed that God had answered her prayer right off. She said, 'How about that! The first person I meet in Winnipeg, and you're a Christian!'"

Smyth had let Carol's narrative run on, but now he interrupted her to ask, "You were the first person she talked to in Winnipeg?"

"Yes, I think so. She said she had just gotten off the plane and taken a taxi right to the house. She still had her suitcases with her in the backyard, I think. I guess Randy hadn't left her a key. Because he didn't know she was coming then, you know."

"What happened next?"

"That's about all. I said I was really glad to meet her, and I was sure we would be good friends. I said I really had to get to that meeting, but I told her my husband Clint was pastor of a new Grace Church starting here, and he would be home any minute. I suggested that when he got here, she should introduce herself and he could tell her more about it. I even suggested that maybe she and Randy could come for supper, but she wasn't sure if Randy would like that. So we said good-bye, but I was sure Clint would be home any minute. In fact, I left Barney out in the yard."

"Who?" said Prestwyck, feeling that somehow the police should be involved with the conversation.

"The dog," Carol said. "We don't usually leave him in the yard because he barks."

"What was Moira wearing?" Smyth asked.

"Wearing? I don't know. I could see only her head and shoulders, but I think she had on a white blouse."

"Was Moira wearing any jewelry?" Smyth asked.

"Yes, I had forgotten that. When I said we were with Grace Church, she started to show me a necklace that someone had given her. I think it was someone from a Grace Church, maybe the person who led her to become a Christian, but I didn't really have time to look at it, because I was late. She really wanted to talk, but I couldn't stay. I told her to show it to Clint when he got here."

Both policemen were starting to watch Clint now, and he fidgeted a bit. "And what did you talk to Moira about when you got home?" Prestwyck asked him.

"I—I didn't," Clint stammered. "I had just phoned Carol

and said I was coming home right away. But since she was going out, I decided to take the long way home, drive around a bit, so I was about a half-hour later than she expected. When I got here, I didn't see anyone next door, but then I wouldn't necessarily because the fence is high. The dog was running around barking in the yard, so I thought I had better take him into the house right away. Anyway, I never met her. In fact, I've never seen her."

"Have you seen her again, Carol?"

"No. I've gone over a couple of times, but Randy always seems so unfriendly. Moira doesn't seem to be around at all. I wondered whether she stayed only a couple of days and then went back to wherever she was before to pack up her stuff."

"But we don't even know where she's from," Clint protested.

"I know," Smyth said.

Four pairs of eyes turned to him.

Smyth reached into the brown envelope and took out a picture. He handed it to Carol. "Is that the necklace she was wearing?"

"Yes, yes it is! See, it says "Grace" on it. Where did you get this?"

Smyth reached into the envelope and brought out the other picture. "Is this Moira?"

"Oh, yes, that's her! But how did you get her picture?"

"That's a good question, Mr. Smyth," said Devorkian.

"These photos were sent to me by Carl Brager of River Valley Grace Church in Minneapolis to go with a story for *Grace* magazine. His wife, Shirley, led Moira to Christ during a Bible study."

"Isn't that wonderful!" Carol exclaimed. "It *was* another Grace church."

"Yes," Smyth continued. "Shirley gave her the 'Grace' pendant, which Moira hung on the chain around her neck.

The pendant was a symbol of the church's personal outreach program—they call it 'Grace to Face'."

"So, Mr. Granowski," Devorkian put in, "it looks like you were the last person to see Moira alive."

"Don't jump to conclusions, Detective," Smyth said. "I believe Clint is telling the truth about never meeting Moira. Before I came to see you tonight, I phoned Shirley Brager and talked to her again about Moira. She didn't know where Moira and her husband were moving, but she did remember Moira had said her husband's name was Randy. Moira also told her that Randy was a drug dealer and maybe involved with organized crime. Moira evidently didn't know for sure, but she was certainly worried what Randy would do when she told him she had become an evangelical Christian. In fact, Shirley suggested that maybe she should just get away from Randy, but Moira said she loved him and wanted an opportunity to tell him about Jesus. She thought maybe she could save him."

"That doesn't necessarily mean that Randy killed her," Prestwyck said.

"No, but remember what I said I saw from the plane. There was a dog running around in the yard next to the one in which I saw the murder. The woman was near the house, facing a man in the backyard, near the garage—where her husband would have parked his car."

Devorkian turned to Prestwyck, "Okay, which one of us is going to ask for the search warrant this time?"

"I just want to know what Scott Ledyear is going to say about this."

"Not to mention Mary Alice Bruckner!"

It was after midnight when Smyth finally got home, but writers learn to seize the moments when thoughts come together—

the moments that some label inspiration. Before going up to bed, he slipped into his tiny basement office, turned on his computer, and typed a rough draft and some notes for his next editorial.

Across the top of the page were the words, “A Woman Named Grace.”

Chapter 19

WEDNESDAY, JULY 24

It was not one of Winnipeg's best restaurants, but the food was good, and John and Ruby Smyth were enjoying it. With a church salary, they didn't get to come to even this class of restaurant very often. They held hands under the table and smiled across at Sergeant Prestwyck and Detective Devorkian.

"We want to thank you for this. It really wasn't necessary."

Prestwyck held up his hand. "It's okay. We wanted to say thank you . . ."

"For not talking to Scott Ledyear," Devorkian put in.

"That really wasn't much of a sacrifice," John said.

Prestwyck continued, "No, I wanted to thank you for bringing in the information when you did. I doubt we would have ever solved the case without that information. I also wanted to apologize for not believing your story at first."

John smiled. "It's okay. I didn't believe it myself at first either." He paused. "Does this mean the case is solved? Did you find much evidence when you searched Randy Campani's house?"

"Not a lot," Prestwyck said, "but enough. There were traces of blood on the back step that matched Moira's DNA, and some tooth chips. There was more blood in the trunk of his car. And there were traces of cloth having been burnt in the fireplace—not much, but we think that is where he burned her clothes."

"Don't forget the fingerprint," said Devorkian.

"Yes. One fingerprint on the back window, where she probably looked in to see if he was home. Her suitcases were also there, in a basement storeroom, with more of her clothes in them and one or two more of her fingerprints—plus Randy's prints on the handle."

"That was rather foolish wasn't it—to keep them?" Ruby asked.

"Not so foolish as you might think," Prestwyck said. "You have to remember that we didn't even find the body for two weeks, and then we couldn't identify it. Campani wasn't even a suspect, so there was little chance we would search his house. Even if we'd arrested him for something else, we wouldn't necessarily have connected the suitcases to the missing woman. And what else could he have done with them? He couldn't just dump them on the side of the road or throw them in the garbage—it might attract too much attention, especially since we were searching for a missing woman. The same with giving the clothes to the Salvation Army, a thrift store, or some place like that. The police might check all those places just in case someone had turned in some clothes. Of course, he could have just dropped them off at the door, but we still might have been able to trace the clothes or the luggage, and the bags themselves might have suggested she was new in town."

"And we did in fact check those places," said Devorkian.

"So you have charged Campani with murder?" John asked.

"Oh, yes," said Prestwyck. "We didn't mention the most important piece of evidence, the gun. It took us a while Friday morning to get the search warrant, and by then Campani had gone out. When he came back, we were waiting for him. He had the gun on him, and the ballistics match the bullet that killed Moira. For what it's worth, we also found drugs in the house. Evidently Campani and his friends were starting a branch office in Winnipeg."

"So Randy killed Moira in the backyard, just as I saw it from the plane?" John asked.

"Looks that way," said Prestwyck. "There is no evidence she ever even got into the house. She had just arrived, and I guess Randy figured he would kill her before she had a chance to talk to anybody."

"But wasn't he taking an awful chance?" Ruby asked.

"Yes," Prestwyck replied, "but he probably figured he'd be taking an even bigger chance by waiting till someone knew she was there and then killing her. Campani is the kind of guy who lives by taking chances. Besides, the sound of the shot would be muffled by the plane flying low overhead."

"He obviously didn't realize Moira had already talked to Carol," Ruby said.

"Yes," Prestwyck replied, "but she wasn't the only witness. We checked the airline records and know she was on the flight from Minneapolis. We also checked the taxi records of her trip to Campani's house. The driver even remembers her—seems she gave him some kind of religious tract."

"That reminds me," Ruby said. "Do you think Moira talked to Randy about becoming a Christian?"

"Who knows?" Prestwyck said. "Campani isn't talking.

She must have said something to make him think he couldn't trust her."

"Why do you care?" Devorkian asked the Smyths. "Why would you want him to become a Christian? You wouldn't really forgive him, would you, after what he did to Moira?"

"It's not up to us to forgive him," John said. "That's up to God—and to Moira. But God wants us to offer his salvation to everyone. As a matter of fact, I think Clint Granowski has already visited him."

"Doesn't make any sense to me," Devorkian said. "Cases like that, I wish we had the death penalty. Still, you know what bothers me?"

"What?" Smyth said.

"The coincidence. You saw the murder from the plane, and you got information from both the Bragers in Minneapolis and the Granowskis here."

"Not quite so surprising if you know the church grapevine," John said. "Still, I see your point. On the other hand, I'm not sure I believe in coincidences."

"There's a lot more I don't believe in," said Devorkian. "You mean someone was looking down on her from the sky? That was you, Smyth, not God."

"Oh, I don't know. Think of it. Moira was an orphan, she had no family and no friends—just a husband who murdered her. But she became a Christian, and even though she lived for only a few days after that, she became part of an international family. She was in Winnipeg only an hour, and already she had found a Christian friend."

"You mean Carol Granowski?"

"Yes."

"Two friends, if you count John," Ruby interjected. "I would say that is clear evidence of God's goodness, God's grace."

"But you didn't stop her from being killed," Devorkian continued.

"No, we didn't stop her from being killed, but we did reveal her killer, and now he's being called to account for his actions. And we will see her again."

"Where? You mean in heaven?"

"Yes. In heaven."

"And I suppose Randy Campani will end up in hell?" Devorkian asked impatiently.

John Smyth shrugged. "Unless he changes, which is—"

"And if he did, would you accept him into heaven?"

"It's not up to us. It's God who decides who gets to heaven. But yes, if he chose to follow Christ, he would be our brother. We would accept him as that, a long-lost brother, and so would Moira. After all, none of us claims to be perfect."

"With the possible exception of Scott Ledyear," said Devorkian.

"And Detective Devorkian," smiled Prestwyck.

A 747 taxied down the runway at Winnipeg airport and lifted into the sky. As it circled and rose, the passengers could see below them the city, rising up from the level prairie like a great pyramid, shimmering in the late evening sun.

James R. Coggins is an award-winning writer and the former editor of Mennonite Brethren Herald, a denominational magazine. He holds a doctorate in history from the University of Waterloo and has published two nonfiction books. He and his wife, Jackie, have two children and live in British Columbia.

More information is available on his web site: www.coggins.ca

SINCE 1894, Moody Publishers has been dedicated to equip and motivate people to advance the cause of Christ by publishing evangelical Christian literature and other media for all ages, around the world. Because we are a ministry of the Moody Bible Institute of Chicago, a portion of the proceeds from the sale of this book go to train the next generation of Christian leaders.

If we may serve you in any way in your spiritual journey toward understanding Christ and the Christian life, please contact us at www.moodypublishers.com.

"All Scripture is God-breathed and is useful for teaching, rebuking, correcting and training in righteousness, so that the man of God may be thoroughly equipped for every good work."

—2 TIMOTHY 3:16, 17

More Suspense Fiction from Moody Publishers

The Second Thief

Meet Tom Ledger. Disillusioned. Bored. In search of comfort and ease. Willing to sell his soul—or at least his employer's most closely guarded secret—to the highest bidder.

ISBN: 0-8024-1707-8

Tom has no way of knowing that within hours of committing his first felony, he'll be catapulted into a high-stakes drama as the airplane he's on drops like a rock into a Nebraska cornfield. But as he faces what could be the final moments of his life, even his pitiful attempt at prayer is self-serving: "Please God, please let me live."

As Tom confronts his past and all its consequences, he has some decisions to make—life-or-death decisions. Will he continue on the path that threatens to destroy everything he once held dear, or can he find another way home?

The Fall

ISBN: 0-8024-1405-2

Good-guy Morris Jackson is content with his life in the gritty urban neighborhood of Quiley Heights. But Quiley Heights is a far cry from paradise. When vivid dreams of a hauntingly beautiful place begin troubling Morris's sleep, the contrast between his idyllic visions and the routine of daily life becomes too much to bear. As his real and dream worlds collide, Morris finds himself caught in a downward spiral, unable to escape the evil forces that threaten him—in the dangerous city streets, in his increasingly frightening dreams, and in the darkest places of his own soul.

Can anyone rescue Morris before he falls beyond recovery?

1-800-678-6928 www.MoodyPublishers.org

Who's Grace? Team

Acquiring Editor:
Michele Straubel

Copy Editor:
Anne Buchanan

Back Cover Copy:
Julie-Allyson Ieron, Joy Media

Cover Design:
UDG DesignWorks

Interior Design:
Ragont Design

Printing and Binding:
Bethany Press International

The typeface for the text of this book is
Fairfield LH